LOVE AT MORLEY COVE

LOVE AT MORLEY COVE

•

Katrina Thomas

AVALON BOOKS
NEW YORK

Published by Avalon Books,
an imprint of Thomas Bouregy & Co., Inc.
160 Madison Avenue, New York, NY 10016

Library of Congress Cataloging-in-Publication Data

Thomas, Katrina, 1959–
   Love at Morley Cove / Katrina Thomas.
      p. cm.
   ISBN 978-0-8034-7714-8 (acid-free paper)   1. Child
rearing—Fiction.   2. North Carolina—Fiction.
I. Title.
   PS3620.H629L68 2011
   813'.6—dc22
                                                    2010031074

PRINTED IN THE UNITED STATES OF AMERICA
ON ACID-FREE PAPER
BY HADDON CRAFTSMEN, BLOOMSBURG, PENNSYLVANIA

To the Schwendy, Monnat,
Thomas, and Morin families—
thank you for the good times, and the challenges, too!

Chapter One

Don't look now, but here comes your prince."

Reine Jonson followed her friend's gaze to the tall man in a dark gray suit striding toward their table on the lawn of the Nags Head Library and Community Center. Even at a distance, she saw that his jaw was set in a firm line while his steps revealed determination and purpose.

"My prince, Deb? Be serious."

"I'm very serious. Stephen Morley is rich and successful *and* handsome."

"He never smiles."

"Does that really matter?"

"Being able to smile about things in your life is much more important than having money."

Her friend waved at the approaching gentleman. "Good morning, Mr. Morley."

Reine watched as his intense dark eyes scanned the table. He looked at the posters attached to the front, the piles of multicolored flyers, and the sign-up sheets before leveling his gaze on her friend. She could not help but notice that his broad shoulders filled his suit jacket perfectly; but despite his confident appearance, he seemed unhappy.

"Hello, Miss Lyons. The choir director mentioned that you may need some assistance with the community youth group's new project."

"How wonderful." Deborah did not hide her delight. "You're one of the first to volunteer."

He stared at the pen and paper she slid toward him. "What exactly does this venture entail?"

Deborah's smile broadened as she pointed to the poster board attached to the front of the table. "Reine and I are chairing the committee to help the youth group update the children's library here at the community center. We've organized some fund-raising activities, including a garage sale during the Summer Fun Days next month. We could certainly use your help."

He lifted dark brows above questioning eyes. *What do you need me to do?*

Reine tried not to show her irritation as she observed the exchange between one of the town's most prominent businessmen and her best friend since kindergarten. *Is he kidding? Is it possible that he does not know how he could help a fund-raising activity? Does Deborah really find the situation so amusing?*

"Of course, *your* help." Deborah laughed. "You may make a donation or volunteer your time. The youth group is collecting good used clothing, household items, books, and furniture. Things that some people don't want or need anymore, but that others may. We're going to sell the donated items here at the community center during the Summer Fun Days in August. Would you like to make a donation?"

He reached into the inside pocket of his jacket and pulled out a leather-covered checkbook. "I'll be happy to write a check for this new project."

Inhaling a deep breath to calm her impatience, Reine decided that it was time she intervened. "We appreciate your generosity,

Mr. Morley, but the committee agreed that we would try to raise money with our time and talent, rather than by simply collecting monetary donations."

The man's dark eyes held hers as though he were seeing her for the first time. She felt a blush rise up on her cheeks as he continued to study her. The intensity of his gaze made her uneasy.

Finally, he spoke. "Am I to understand that you are declining my offer, Miss—?"

"Jonson," Deborah said as she grasped Reine's arm. "She just means that the members of the youth group want to raise the money for new library books from activities they've planned to hold throughout the summer."

He continued to look at Reine. "It has always been my belief that a donation check could be used to buy a great many items, including those to update a library."

Are you being obstinate on purpose, Mr. Morley? Reine squared her shoulders as she ignored her burning cheeks. "The youth group decided that they would like to focus on *working* to raise money rather than just collecting it. They want to give their free time and use their individual skills to come up with the necessary funds."

"Yes," Deborah said with a nod and a smile. "Perhaps you have an old table or chest you're no longer using. Someone in town may need something that you don't."

"Some of the kids are collecting and pricing items for the garage sale. Others are mowing lawns or offering to go shopping or to run errands for people."

Deborah's head bobbed up and down. "It's like you being in the community outdoor choir, Mr. Morley."

His eyebrows rose higher. "I fail to see the connection."

"You go to rehearsals and sing at every performance. You use your wonderful baritone voice to entertain and inspire people. You don't *have* to practice after a long day of work. You don't *have* to sing those solo parts, but you do. You use your singing skills and give your time to be a part of the community."

"Exactly." Reine sighed. She was relieved to know that her friend was finally helping her to make her point with the stubborn man standing in front of them. Using his membership in the choir as an analogy was perfect. "You don't write a check and say, 'Hire people with talented voices to sing for the next concert.' You use your *own* time and talent."

Watching a shadow cross his face, she wondered if she had gone too far in trying to persuade him to understand her side of the issue. It was not the first time she had annoyed someone with her persistence.

"So, is there an old piece of furniture at that big house of yours that you'd like to donate to our cause?"

"I'm afraid I replace my furniture when it gets old, Miss Jonson; and I discard worn clothing as soon as I no longer want it. I do not think I will be able to help you. As for what you call my talent, I am afraid I have to resign from the community choir."

"Resign? Oh, Mr. Morley, you can't." Deborah jumped up from her seat. "The summer outdoor concerts at the park pavilion just won't be the same without you."

"Thank you, but I'm afraid I must. It is unavoidable. I have other . . . obligations."

"The choir needs you."

The quiet ring of a telephone sounded, and Stephen Morley pulled the small device from the waistband of his trousers. "Please excuse me, ladies."

"Let us know if you can help," Deborah called after the tall, retreating figure. Then she turned to Reine. "He would be just perfect for you."

"You've got to be kidding."

"I wonder why he's not dating anyone." Deborah wrinkled her nose. "Oh, swat that thing, will you?"

Reine followed the direction of her friend's shaking finger as it pointed at a dragonfly on her shoulder. She cupped the insect in her hands and leaned down to set it on the ground. "How do you know he's not?"

"Yuk!" Deborah eyed the dragonfly and shivered. "Because I've asked around. He works too hard and spends his evenings alone. He needs someone caring like you who can teach him how to relax and to enjoy life. Why do you think he's resigning from the choir?"

"He said he had obligations. Summer is the busiest time of year on the Outer Banks. I'm sure the Morley Cove Resort takes up all of his time right now."

"There's always time for dating, especially when you've found the right one."

Her friend's eyes sparkled with apparent assurance that she knew what was best for Reine, but volunteers began to approach the table to sign up for the upcoming library fund-raiser, and she had no chance to respond to Deborah's remark. She was too busy greeting both year-round members of the community and summer residents, as well as passing out flyers, to think about Stephen Morley for the remainder of the morning.

As she and Deborah began to clear the table a few hours later, she was surprised to see her brother hurrying across the lawn of the Nags Head Library and Community Center. She smiled at Niles, who was dressed in faded jeans and the T-shirt she had given him from the University of North Carolina a few years ago.

"Reine, I thought you'd left already. I didn't see your car. Where'd you park it?"

She sighed. "It's at Don's garage getting fixed. I walked."

Niles shook his head as he reached for the poster in her hand. "Can't you just get a new one? The poor old thing always needs some part repaired or replaced."

Reine piled flyers and slipped them into her worn canvas

bag. "I can hardly afford the repairs it needs. How can I possibly come up with money for the down payment on a new car?"

"I can help you."

"As usual, Niles, I appreciate the offer, but I'm not taking money from my big brother." She pushed the handles of the bag over her shoulder. "You don't look like you're dressed for Grandma's Sunday pot roast dinner."

"Well, the offer's open when you stop being so stubborn." Niles handed her the poster. "Anyway, about dinner. That's why I'm here. I have to take a charter out this afternoon, so I won't be able to eat with you. Will you tell Grandpa and Grandma I'm sorry? They were still at church when I left, or I would have told them myself."

"You're working today? Since when do you charter trips on Sunday?"

He stuffed his hands into the front pockets of his jeans. "It's not something I plan to make a habit of, but I got a special request to take a guest from Morley Cove Resort out to the Gulf Stream for an afternoon of deep-sea fishing. The guy has to return to Chicago tomorrow and was really looking forward to catching something before he left."

With a stack of papers in her hands, Deborah rounded the table. "I heard a rumor that Morley Cove was getting rid of their charter boat."

Niles shrugged. "Their captain just had to resign because of some family problems. Stephen Morley called personally to ask me to take this guest out."

Deborah whistled. "Imagine! Reine's future husband asking you to help him."

Niles grinned at Reine. "Really? I didn't even know you were interested in him."

Reine gave her best friend a warning glance before she shook her head. "I'm not. Why don't you stop fantasizing about me and use your energy to find your own true love?"

Deborah grinned. "Oh, I'm working on that too."

"I'd love to stay and chat about your romantic prospects, but I have to get going. Do you need a ride back to Grandpa and Grandma's?"

Reine shook her head. "No, I don't mind the walk. It's a beautiful day."

Niles glanced up at the clear, cloudless sky. "I hope the fish are biting. I don't want Morley's guest to be disappointed."

"Be careful out there on the water."

"I will. I promise."

After Reine and Deborah returned the table to the storage building, they fell into step next to each other along the sidewalk in front of the community center. The sun was already hot, but a refreshing breeze from the ocean tempered the heat to a comfortable level.

"I'm serious about your dismal love life, Reine. It's time you started thinking about your future."

"I am thinking about it." She sighed. "As soon as I raise enough money for a down payment on a new car, I can start saving again for graduate courses."

"I don't mean your *career* future, dummy. I mean your *real* future, with a commitment to someone." Deborah blew out a puff of air. "You know what I mean. Your own family. Your children."

"I don't know if that's the life I want, Deb."

"Of course it is, Reine. Just look at your grandparents. They have a wonderful, close relationship. You can't let your bad experience with Alan Smythe ruin your attitude about all men. He was scum from the start. He only wanted to go out with you because you're pretty and quiet. He didn't figure on your having a brain or an opinion or two. That's why he broke up with you. He couldn't stand to date someone smarter than he is."

"He left without saying goodbye. It's been over a year, Deb, and I haven't heard a single word from him."

"And good riddance to him." Her friend brushed the palms of her hands for emphasis. "Come on. Be honest. You haven't really missed the creep, have you?"

Reine turned the corner and Deborah followed her. "I suppose not, but I feel like such a fool for thinking he actually liked me."

They headed down a quiet street lined with weathered cedar trees and scraggy shrubs two blocks inland from Roanoke Sound. The soft, humid breeze blew across Reine's arms as she realized that she had not thought about Alan Smythe in months.

"Don't worry. Alan clearly wasn't your type. He favored strawberry ice cream, didn't he?"

Reine stopped and looked at her friend. "I don't remember. Why?"

Deborah nodded. "Stephen Morley is the one for you. In fact, I'm sure of it."

"What are you talking about?"

They began to walk again. "He likes plain vanilla, just like you."

"You're making absolutely no sense to me, Deb."

"No, listen, I have this theory."

Reine stopped in front of the sand and gravel drive of her grandparents' small, white wooden house with dark green shutters. "I'm afraid you'll have to tell me about it later. I promised Grandma I'd help her prepare the meal today. Are you sure you don't want to stay and eat with us?"

Deborah shook her head. "My parents are waiting for me. We're going down to Cape Hatteras for the day for a family picnic. But don't think we're finished with this conversation."

Reine smiled. Now, why would she think that? Deborah was not one to let go of an idea she felt strongly about, and it appeared that Stephen Morley was on her list of current interests.

*   *   *

When Reine arrived at work Monday morning, she was still thinking about Deborah's ice cream theory and wondering how she would pay for the repairs on her ten-year-old car. She walked past an exhibit of watercolor paintings by a local artist before turning left into her office at the Nags Head Library and Community Center.

As she entered the back of the building, she smiled at her assistant. "Hello, Eleanor. I hope your weekend went well."

She set her large canvas bag on the desk covered with stacks of ongoing research she was doing on local family histories and walked to the nearby table. Pouring a mug of coffee from the glass pot, she reached for the pile of messages Eleanor handed her.

"My weekend was great, and the weather was wonderful. I hope it's just as nice for the Summer Fun Days next month."

Reine sipped the strong, hot liquid as she shuffled through the pink slips of paper. "People always seem to have a good time, whether it's sunny or not."

She stopped speaking and stared at the message on top of the pile in her hand. She lifted her gaze to Eleanor. "What's this?"

The older woman rounded a table piled with books and slid her reading glasses up onto her nose. "Oh, Stephen Morley. He's called twice this morning."

The image of the man's intense dark eyes and unsmiling face flashed through Reine's mind as she heard his name. "Stephen Morley called for me?"

"Why, yes." Eleanor pulled off her glasses and let them dangle around her neck. "The phone was ringing when I arrived at eight, and then he called again just a few minutes ago. He seemed quite insistent that he speak with you."

"Insistent? About what?"

"I'm not sure. He didn't say, but he asked me to tell you that he would like you to call him at your earliest convenience."

Chapter Two

Reine stared at the pile of messages in her hand. Stephen Morley had called *two* times. She could think of no possible reason why the prominent businessman would be contacting her.

Maybe he had found something to donate for the youth group garage sale. That could be it.

She looked up at Eleanor and smiled. "What's on today's schedule?"

"Pierre Baxter from Hatteras Island is coming at two to talk about his book on Native American tribes of the Outer Banks. The Dancing Stitches Club will be here at four to set up their display of heirloom pattern quilts."

Reine nodded. "I may have to run over to Don Jenkins' garage for a short while this morning. Do you mind handling things while I'm gone?"

"No problem."

In the stack of papers in Reine's hand, there was no message from the mechanic who was working on her car. Perhaps that was a good sign. Maybe her vehicle was repaired and ready for her to drive. Although the two calls from Stephen Morley intrigued her, she was more interested in whether or not she would have to use her next year's salary to replace her only means of transportation, except, of course, her even older ten-speed bicycle.

She rounded the corner of her desk and dialed the number of Don's garage. He answered on the first ring.

"Hey, Reine, I was just about to call you. I'm afraid I don't have good news."

"I definitely need a new transmission?"

"And an alternator and brakes and routers. I can have Craig start on it this morning, but I wanted to check with you first. It's going to cost you quite a bit of money."

Reine sighed. "How much?"

"Too much. You should look into replacing it. I can give you a discount on the parts because you're such a loyal customer, Reine, and I can set up a payment plan, but you really should consider getting another car."

"I hate paying on credit."

"I know you do, but I'm guessing you don't have that kind of money just sitting around."

No, you're right. I don't. She switched the receiver to her other ear. "Can you start with the brakes? I have enough saved for those. I'll need a few days to come up with a plan to pay for the rest of the repairs."

"Sure. You just let me know when. I'll park it in a bay we don't use very often and wait till you call."

"Thanks, Don." Her shoulders dropped, and her chest tightened as she hung up the telephone. She'd known the mechanic would have bad news. Where was she going to get that much money? With unsteady fingers, she unfolded the creased pile of messages in her hand and shuffled through them.

Stephen Morley's name on one of the message notes caught her attention once again. She picked up the receiver and dialed the number Eleanor had written on the paper. Maybe hearing that he had a donation for the garage sale would help lift her spirits.

A cheerful male voice answered, and the person identified himself as Terry Deacon, Mr. Morley's secretary at Morley Cove Resort. "Yes, Miss Jonson. Mr. Morley is eager to speak with you. Let me see if he is available to take your call."

Eager to tell me about some piece of furniture he wants to donate? While she waited to hear Stephen Morley's quiet baritone voice over the telephone, she pictured in her mind his sad, dark eyes and determined jawline. She wondered if a joyful smile ever smoothed the angular features of his handsome face.

"Miss Jonson, thank you for returning my call. I'm afraid I have a full schedule this morning. Would you be able to meet with me at my office this afternoon?"

Meet with you? This afternoon? Surely, Stephen Morley would not request to meet with her to tell her about a simple donation to the community fund-raising event, would he?

She wadded the pile of messages in her hand again. "I finish work at five. I could stop by after I leave today."

"Five will be fine. Just give Terry a call when you're on your way."

"I'm trading half of my ham and cheese for half of your lettuce and tomato."

Deborah handed Reine a plastic sandwich bag as a foam-edged wave rushed up the beach toward them. Bright, hot streams of summer sun heated the quiet oceanside park overlooking the Atlantic. "You need a little protein in your diet while you're trying to save money for graduate school."

Reine sighed as she nibbled a piece of seedless watermelon. "I'm going to have to put that dream on hold again for a while."

Her friend replaced a leaf of lettuce that had slid out from between the two pieces of whole wheat bread. "Did you get the repair estimate from Don?"

Reine stared out at the huge expanse of water and marveled at how small and powerless she felt at that moment. "Including parts and labor, it will be more than a few paychecks. That's with a discount."

Deborah swallowed a bite of sandwich. "Well, what do you expect? Don's been holding the poor thing together with wire and duct tape for years now."

"I was hoping it would last a couple of years longer. I really wanted to start graduate school in September."

She watched a seagull swoop toward the surface of the water. A sailboat with a blue and yellow sail floated past them.

"What are you going to do?"

"I don't know yet." Reine wrapped her uneaten half of sandwich in waxed paper and put it back in her lunch bag. "But I have to come up with a plan soon."

"You know, Reine, if you didn't do so much volunteer work researching those genealogies, you might be able to afford a few extras for yourself, including a new car."

"Researching is part of my job at the library. People may make a donation, but I'm not allowed to charge them for the information I collect for them."

Deborah shook her head. "I'm not talking about the studies you do on Outer Banks history. I think it's a shame that you do all that research on ancestry and background of individual families, and they pay you nothing for your time."

Reine took a drink from a bottle of spring water. "I enjoy exploring family trees."

"And you're really good at it, so why shouldn't you get paid for it? You do it at home, on your own time, with your own computer. It's not actually part of your job at the library and community center. I think you should start charging people for all the work you do."

Reine searched for another conversation topic. "Stephen Morley called this morning."

Deborah stared at her. "What did you say?"

"He wants to meet with me after work."

"About what? What's going on, Reine?"

"I have no idea. Maybe he has a donation. I can't think of any other reason why he would be contacting me."

"I can't believe he'd actually ask to meet with you about a piece of old furniture." Deborah grinned. "I think Stephen Morley called you because he likes you. You're perfect for him."

"I'm not even considering such an absurd possibility."

"It's not so absurd. You both like plain vanilla ice cream."

"Oh, come on. Not that again."

Deborah met Reine's glare with a sheepish grin. "I have connections. He stops for a treat at the Creamy Scoop on his way home from work once or twice a week. Lucy Ames, the manager there, told me he always gets a hand-packed half pint of plain vanilla ice cream."

"Deborah Lyons!"

"What? I'm only looking out for your best interest."

"I don't see how your spying on Stephen Morley is in *my* best interest."

"Well, it is. I just know the two of you were made for each other. You both like plain vanilla."

"What does that have to do with anything?"

"You like vanilla. He likes vanilla. It's simple. You were meant to be together."

"What a ridiculous suggestion, Deborah. People do not become attracted to each other because they like the same flavor of ice cream."

"I read a book that described how ice cream flavor preference is a true sign of compatibility."

Reine shook her head. "You need to stop. Stephen Morley and I hardly know each other. Anyway, I believe that fate brings a man and a woman together in a committed relationship, not ice cream."

"Oh, destiny plays a part, but the ice cream theory makes sense. Guess who likes my favorite ice cream, mocha almond crunch?"

"Don't tell me Lucy keeps track of that for you too."

Her best friend nodded. "Jeremy Lawson. Two scoops in a waffle cone every Saturday after his nephew's Little League game."

"Jeremy Lawson, my brother's friend from high school? The Jeremy Lawson who works at Morley Cove Resort? The Director of Guest Affairs there?"

Deborah tossed her empty snack bag of potato chips into a nearby trash can and wiped her fingers on a napkin. "That's the one. I'm meeting him at the Creamy Scoop on Wednesday after we finish collecting donations. You're still helping, right? Why don't you come with me?"

Reine zipped her nylon lunch bag. "I don't think so."

"Oh, it'll be fun. Maybe I can see if Jeremy will ask his boss to come too. We could double-date."

Reine stared at her friend. "Absolutely not. Don't you dare."

Deborah shrugged. "If he's still following his routine, he'll be stopping by anyway."

Reine knew she shouldn't encourage her friend's imagination, but she couldn't help being curious. "What do you mean *if* he's still following it?"

"Stephen Morley is shrouded in anonymity." Deborah repacked her own lunch bag and finished her can of soda. "There's something very puzzling about him. He came to Nags Head to take over the management of Morley Cove Resort three years ago and moved onto his family's secluded property just up the waterfront on Roanoke Sound. He tore down the old fishing bungalow on the edge of the cove and built a huge, brand-new beach house."

Reine nodded. "I've seen it. What a gorgeous place!"

"Four floors. Ten bedrooms. Nine baths." Deborah flung her arms out in front of her. "What does he do with all that space? Where's the rest of his family? He spends most of his time working. He never entertains people, and he rarely eats out. The only activity he's been participating in is singing in the outdoor community choir, and now he's resigned from that. Don't you ever wonder why he lives in such solitude?"

Deborah continued to talk as she and Reine left the small public park next to the beach. "What obligations could make him resign his membership? He has such a wonderful voice. It's a shame he has to quit." Deborah shook her head. "And today, when Mrs. Saunders went to the store for his groceries, she bought bananas and two bottles of fruit juice."

Reine stopped and stared at her. Deborah's job as head manager of the Oceanfront Market, a combination grocery and hardware store, had always been a good place for her friend to hear about news of the local residents and tourists alike.

"You keep track of his groceries? Really, Deb!"

"No, listen, Reine. This is very interesting. Now, those items wouldn't be unusual for most people. For instance, Mr. McClure buys apple juice three times a week. Miss Manning gets a bottle of grape and one of cranberry every Saturday. Even Mrs. Saunders gets juice now and then, but she wasn't shopping for herself today. She goes to the market every Monday morning to buy Stephen Morley's groceries."

Reine nodded. "His housekeeper. Yes, I've heard she works for him, but you still haven't explained about the bananas."

Deborah shook her head. "Mrs. Saunders has never, in the three years since Stephen Morley hired her, purchased a single banana. Today, she bought a whole bunch of them. And she bought a bottle of apple juice and one of grape and three boxes of breakfast cereal. *Three* boxes of sweetened breakfast cereal."

Reine waited for cars to pass before crossing the busy street full of tourist traffic coming from the mainland of North Carolina. Deborah hurried to catch up with her.

"There's quite a mystery developing here."

Reine stopped near the entrance of the Oceanfront Market. "The only mystery is how you manage to keep your life in order when you're so busy snooping into everyone else's."

Deborah reached for the door handle and grinned. "And I still can't figure out why she bought the half gallon of chocolate ripple ice cream. Stephen likes vanilla."

With a smile and a shake of her head, Reine waved before heading down the block to the Nags Head Library and Community Center. "I'll see you later, Sherlock."

Despite Reine's continuous worry about how she would pay for her car repairs and her growing curiosity about Stephen Morley's request to meet with her, she forced herself to keep her attention on her work. The afternoon passed without any further complications in her usually uncomplicated life. At five minutes after five, she telephoned the executive office at Morley Cove Resort to tell Stephen Morley's secretary that she was on her way.

"I'm afraid there has been a change in Mr. Morley's schedule, Miss Jonson."

A change? She recognized the voice of Terry Deacon. "He has to take care of a minor personal problem, and he apologizes for having to cancel his meeting with you this afternoon. Would it be possible to reschedule?"

A minor personal problem? Won't Deb have fun with that one? She smiled to herself. "Well, yes, of course. Do you know when he'll be available?"

"How is Thursday at five-thirty?"

"I'll be there."

She almost asked the question that had been nagging at her all day. Why did Stephen Morley want to meet with her? She did not know if she could wait for three more days to discover the answer. With a sigh, she replaced the receiver and packed her bag to go home.

"I shouldn't be going for ice cream, Deb. I'm so dusty and dirty."

Her friend parked the loaded station wagon in the gravel parking area and turned off the ignition. "You look fine. Just brush off your shorts and T-shirt with your hands."

"I should have brought a change of clothes with me."

"Oh, stop worrying. We're just going to have a quick dish before we start unloading this stuff. Wow, we got a ton of donations tonight."

Reine hurried to catch up with Deborah as she headed toward the side entrance of the Creamy Scoop Ice Cream and Deli Shop. "We're meeting Jeremy, aren't we?"

"Oh, come on. It's not like he hasn't seen both of us in all stages of untidiness." Deborah grinned as she held open the door, and a blast of cool air blew across Reine's face. "He's still the same old Jeremy, even though it won't be long before he's my one and only." She grabbed Reine's arm. "Look, there he is, over by the make-your-own-sundae bar."

The tall, curly-haired man glanced their way from across the busy restaurant and waved at them. Deborah squealed and tightened her grip on Reine's arm.

"Isn't he handsome? Come on. Let's go say hi before we order."

A few minutes later, they received their ice cream on a plastic tray, and Jeremy carried it to a booth where Reine slid into a seat next to Deborah. After setting two bowls of mocha almond crunch and one of vanilla, along with a stack of paper napkins, on the table, Jeremy sat down across from them.

"It's awfully nice of you to help us unload the garage sale donations, Jeremy." Reine dipped a plastic spoon into her bowl.

"We're always looking for new volunteers at the community center."

"Deb persuaded me." He glanced at Deborah and smiled. "I'm happy to help out."

Reine was about to comment on her own experience with Deborah Lyons' exceptional skills of persuasion when Deb jabbed her elbow into Reine's side. "Okay, okay. I promise I won't say another word."

"No, not that, silly. Look who just walked in."

Reine turned toward the front door. For a moment, a couple pushing a stroller with a squirming toddler obstructed her view, and then she saw him. Stephen Morley weaved his way around a group of customers reading the menu printed on the wall and approached the counter.

His dark business suit looked fresh and wrinkle-free even though he had most likely worn it all day. A frown formed around his mouth, and his jaw was set in the same determined line that Reine had noticed on Sunday. Was he ever happy?

As she studied him, he turned and met her gaze. Intense, sad eyes stared at her, and she swallowed. Maybe he didn't recognize her.

Strands of hair had escaped the elastic band at her nape. Her clothes were creased, and she needed a shower. What a time for her to see Stephen Morley.

With a sinking feeling in the pit of her stomach, she watched him nod and walk toward their booth. *Oh, no.*

"Well, Mr. Morley." Deborah smiled and waved as he approached. "It's nice to see you out on such a beautiful night."

"Hello, Miss Lyons. Miss Jonson. Good evening."

"Why don't you scoot over, Jeremy, and let Mr. Morley sit down."

Stephen Morley appeared to notice his employee for the first time. "Jeremy?"

Jeremy grinned and slid over toward the window. "Please join us, Stephen."

Reine watched him shake his head. "I can't stay. I'm just waiting for my order."

"Plain vanilla, right?"

Reine sent her friend a warning glance. She'd hoped Deborah would keep her embarrassing comments to herself.

His puzzled expression told her he did not understand Deborah's question. Then the gloomy look returned to his face. Reine wondered if anything ever washed the sadness from his eyes.

"You could sit with us while you wait," Jeremy said. "You're not just leaving your office now, are you?"

Stephen nodded. "The air conditioning in the east wing stopped, and I wanted to make sure all the guests were moved to other rooms before I left."

"Why didn't you page me? I would have gone back to help you."

Stephen shook his head. "It was unnecessary to interrupt your plans. I'm glad to see you out enjoying the evening."

"I'm helping Deb and Reine unload donations for their community center fund-raiser."

Reine's heart fluttered when he turned his eyes to hers. She wished she had taken time to run a comb through her hair. "Ah, the Summer Fun Days garage sale. How are the donations coming along?"

"Wonderfully." Deborah reached in front of Reine for a napkin. "We picked up a whole carload tonight."

As Reine attempted to slide the pile toward her friend, she bumped the edge of her bowl. To her dismay, it spun and then fell into her lap before dropping to the floor at Stephen Morley's feet.

She felt her cheeks burn with humiliation as she leaned

down to retrieve the overturned plastic bowl. She misjudged the distance and bumped her head on the edge of the table.

"Are you all right?"

His quiet question made her heart flutter again as she rubbed her head where she had bumped it. All she could do was nod at him. What a mess!

He bent his long legs and, with deft hands, picked up the bowl of vanilla ice cream and wiped the floor with a napkin. After disposing of everything in a nearby trash container, he turned back toward the table. "I'll order you another."

"No, thank you." Reine shook her head. Why had she let Deborah talk her into going to the Creamy Scoop? She wished she was home.

A girl behind the counter gestured to him that his order was ready. He raised his brows at Reine. "Are you sure?"

"Yes, she'll take another bowl of just plain vanilla."

Reine could not believe that Deborah was answering for her. She was already completely humiliated.

"That's her favorite, plain vanilla with nothing on it."

Chapter Three

Thursday afternoon, Reine was helping some volunteers arrange a display of turn-of-the-century photographs of summer residents on the Outer Banks when Eleanor told her she had a telephone call from Don Jenkins. Her stomach twisted in a nervous knot as she hurried to her desk to answer it.

"Reine, I'm glad I caught you before you headed home."

"I hope you have good news, Don."

"I'm afraid not. Short of a miracle or a surprise inheritance from a long-lost relative, I don't think I could give you good news, at least not about that old car of yours. We replaced the brakes and routers, but you need an alignment before you can drive anywhere. In addition to the transmission problems, your two rear tires have almost no tread and need to be replaced before inspection time comes around next month."

Reine groaned. "Please. Don't say anymore."

"Maybe you should start thinking about getting another vehicle. I could look around for a good, reliable used one for you, if you want."

She shifted the receiver to her other ear. "But then I'll have to take out another loan. I can barely make my college loan payment every month. Let me think about it. Thanks for calling, Don."

Reine chewed her lower lip as she ended the call. She was still holding the receiver when it rang, and she jumped.

"This is Terry Deacon. I'm calling at Mr. Morley's request."

"I'm packing up to leave work right now."

"Well, that's why I'm telephoning. He has just been summoned home to take care of a small problem and was wondering if you would be so kind as to meet him at his house on Morley Cove Road."

Another problem at home? What's going on there? "I hope everything is all right. Perhaps we should postpone our meeting?"

"Oh, no. I understand that it is just a slight family matter. Are you familiar with the Morley property?"

"Yes, I know where it is."

Stephen Morley's beach house was a four-story wooden structure built on a narrow piece of property covered with sand, tall grasses, and thick shrubs. Three sides of the land edged the smooth waters of Roanoke Sound between the larger sounds of Albemarle and Pamlico that separated North Carolina's Outer Banks from the mainland. The fourth side was lined with a grove of low, wind-worn oak and pine trees.

The house poked above the treetops as she pedaled her bicycle around the unpaved semicircular drive to the front door. Each of the four floors had numerous windows, glass doors, and wraparound decks and porches. Balconies, outdoor staircases, and cupolas added enchanting detail to the building.

Reine used her toe to release the kickstand of her bicycle and set it against the trunk of a weathered oak tree. The whole place was immense, and she felt small and insignificant as she approached.

Ascending the wide wooden steps leading to the front entrance of the house, she watched the door swing open. A tall, slender woman in a dark skirt and jacket appeared. Her cheeks were flushed, and she was frowning.

"I cannot remain here a moment longer, Mr. Morley."

The woman turned then so her back was to the doorway as a small boy grasped her hand. Tears streamed down his pale cheeks.

"Please don't go, Miss Amber. We took the snake back outside."

At that moment, Stephen Morley strode toward the young woman. He struggled to hold a squirming child in his arms while an older boy stood next to him shuffling his feet.

The child at his side looked up at him. "It was only a little grass snake, Uncle Stephen. We really didn't mean to scare her."

Uncle Stephen?

Reine watched Mr. Morley turn his attention to the woman near the door. His jaw was set in a determined line as he attempted to quiet the whimpering child in his arms while focusing his concentration on the other adult in the hall.

"A snake? That's what this is all about? Surely we can resolve this problem, Miss Eddleton."

He narrowed his intense, dark eyes and looked at the young boy beside him. "I'll see to it that Peter apologizes and makes amends."

The young woman shook her head as the other little boy holding her hand continued to cry. "That's not it, Mr. Morley. Finding that snake on the tea tray was simply the last indignation I am willing to endure. I cannot live here a minute longer."

She threw her arms into the air and set the crying child off balance. On unsteady legs, he wobbled and then fell to the floor.

His screams pierced the air as the little girl Mr. Morley was holding joined him in a chorus of unhappy cries. Reine watched in silent wonder as the upset woman continued to speak in a voice just a little louder than the children's screams.

"How can I be expected to live under such conditions? There is nothing here for me. We are miles from civilization. Two days ago, I was living in a wonderful apartment overlooking Central Park. I was close to stores and culture and human beings. Coming here to take care of three children was a mistake. I thought I could live in this barren, uninhabitable place, but I cannot. I must leave."

Stephen Morley shifted the crying child from one arm to the other. With a frown, he glanced down at the boy still crying on the floor. "Now, Miss Eddleton, I think we should discuss—"

"There is nothing to discuss, Mr. Morley. I have already made up my mind." The sound of approaching footsteps caught Reine's attention. With a large suitcase in each hand, a woman Reine recognized as the housekeeper, Ruth Saunders, hurried toward the group.

"Here are your things, Miss Eddleton. I packed them as quickly as I could." She set the luggage on the hardwood floor and turned to her employer. "Please excuse me, Mr. Morley. I have to go to the kitchen and check on the pies I'm baking."

With tight, unsmiling lips, he nodded at the same moment as a car horn honked. The crying of the children did not stop and actually seemed to increase in volume.

Reine turned as a taxi pulled up to the front steps. She ascended in a hurry and moved to the side to get out of the way.

"That is my cab. You have my address. Just forward my pay to me in New York. I'll be staying with my parents until I find other employment."

"Miss Eddleton, wait—"

Stephen Morley stopped in mid-sentence and stared at Reine. For the first time since she had arrived, he seemed to realize that she was standing there on the porch by the front door of his house. His expression of surprise told her he did not immediately recall why she was waiting in the midst of such chaos.

As Amber Eddleton struggled to lift the heavy suitcases, his eyes darted from Reine to the departing woman. He looked back at Reine again and then held the little girl in his arms out to her.

"Here, please take this child for a moment."

Startled, Reine fumbled to secure the screaming, squirming little girl in her arms. Unfortunately, the child did not appear to like the movement or the change in her position, and her screams increased in intensity.

Stephen Morley stepped over the crying child rocking back and forth on the porch. The boy covered his ears and cried even louder than the little girl. Reine watched Stephen shake his head, grasp the suitcases, and follow Amber Eddleton down the steps to the waiting taxi.

Reine tried to hold on to the wriggling child as the older boy tugged on her sleeve. When she looked down at him, his blue eyes were full of concern.

"She likes it when you pat her back."

"What?" Above the noise of the two crying children, Reine could hear only part of what he'd said.

He cupped his hands around his mouth. "I said, my sister likes to have her back patted. She'll probably quiet down if you walk around with her and pat her back."

Reine smoothed the child's pink cotton knit shirt and hummed a tune her mother used to sing to her when she was a child. Patting the little girl's back with slow, gentle movements, she walked toward the front door of Stephen Morley's beach house and stepped onto the polished hardwood floor of the spacious hall. The child in her arms hiccupped and sighed before setting her blond head on Reine's shoulder.

The older boy grinned up at her. "Sarah doesn't usually get quiet that fast."

Reine glanced back at the smaller boy, whose own cries had turned to soft whimpers. As she watched, he pulled his hands from his ears and met her eyes with his large blue ones.

"I don't want Miss Amber to leave. It was just a little snake."

The older boy held out his hand to the younger one and pulled the child to his feet. "Just because we want a pet doesn't mean everybody does, Jonah. But I still can't figure out how that snake got on the tea tray." The older boy's face had a puzzled expression.

The younger child kicked the floor with the toe of his sneaker. "Chester likes to curl around warm things like the teapot. I just wanted him to be happy."

"You put him there? You put Chester on Miss Amber's tea tray? Oh, we're in big trouble now. Uncle Stephen is really mad."

The two boys stepped into the hall and turned to Reine as the older one held out his hand. "I'm Peter Morley, and this is my brother Jonah. You're holding our sister, Sarah."

With care, Reine removed a hand from around the now dozing child in her arms and shook Peter's outstretched one. "I'm very happy to meet you. My name is Reine."

Jonah tipped his head and studied her. "Rain, like the rain on a stormy day?"

She smiled at the blond boy. "It sounds the same, just a different spelling."

"Reine. I like that, and I think Sarah likes *you*. Are you going to take care of us now that Miss Amber is leaving?"

"Oh, no, I'm just here to meet with Mr. . . . , I mean, your uncle."

Jonah's bottom lip began to tremble as he peered out the open door. Stephen Morley and Amber Eddleton appeared to be having an animated conversation while the cab waited in the driveway.

Jonah tipped his head up at her. "Do you have time to read us a story?"

"Jonah likes the picture book about the puppies on the farm. Miss Amber was going to read it right after tea at four-thirty. She's English, you know."

Reine looked at the two sets of large blue eyes pleading with her. "Yes, I guess I have time to read one story. Will your sister get upset it I sit down?"

"Not if you rock her." Jonah clutched her elbow and steered her toward a doorway on the left side of the hall.

She stepped into a formal living room with pale green upholstered sofas and chairs and a wall of large windows overlooking Roanoke Sound. In one corner of the room, a white wooden rocker and a small couch faced a stone fireplace.

As Reine looked around at the simple yet elegant furnishings, she recalled Stephen Morley's remark on Sunday that he had no unnecessary pieces of furniture at his house. In the living room, at least, there did not seem to be a single item that did not fit the inviting décor.

Jonah led her to the rocker. "You sit here with Sarah. I'll get the puppy story."

She rubbed the little girl's back as the child in her arms made restless movements against her. "Are you sure she won't wake up?"

Peter shook his head. "It's her nap time. She should sleep for a while."

Jonah rushed back from a bookcase at the other end of the room. "I got the big truck story and one about penguins too." He held out a book to her as she sat down in the rocker and settled Sarah against her left shoulder.

He flopped down on his stomach on the area rug in front of her while Peter sat cross-legged next to his brother. In silence, both boys turned expectant eyes toward her.

Reine inhaled a deep breath and flipped through the pages

of the picture book full of colorful illustrations and paragraphs of text. *What am I doing here?*

Questions raced through her mind as she positioned the book in her right hand and turned to the first page. As she read, she pushed the floor with the tip of her shoe to set the rocker in motion. The slow, smooth movements relaxed her, and she felt a sense of calm surround her, one she had not experienced all week.

The sleeping child on her lap sighed and snuggled against her. The boys on the floor in front of her listened with polite attention.

At the conclusion of the story, she smiled at the surprise ending. The puppy solved his problem. All the animals were happy. It was a perfect story.

"Now read the penguin one please." Jonah lifted an arm from the rug to hand her another large picture book. "This one's even better. Someday I'm going to go to Antarctica and study the penguins there."

"I'm going to stay right here and be like Uncle Stephen," Peter said. "I'm going to have a big office and work really hard and be busy all the time, just like him."

Jonah tipped his blond head to one side, as though he were giving his brother's plan serious consideration. "I don't think that's a good idea. Uncle Stephen's not happy. Don't you want to be happy when you grow up, Peter?"

The sound of someone clearing his throat caught Reine's attention. She turned her focus from the exchange between the two small boys to their uncle in a tailored suit and polished leather loafers striding across the living room floor toward them.

She watched his intense eyes survey the scene before him as she studied the unreadable expression on his tanned, angular face. Again, she noticed his strong jawline and the resolute determination in his steps. When he stopped just inches from the edge of the rug on which his nephews sat, she could not deny the power and strength he exuded in his stance.

Her gaze rose to meet his probing eyes. She almost forgot about the child in her arms until the little girl whimpered in her sleep.

"Miss Jonson, I'm sorry for imposing on you like this. Let me take the child."

"Here you are." Ruth Saunders entered the room as she smoothed the front of her white cotton apron. "The pies are cooling, and I'll be glad to watch the children now."

The housekeeper turned to look at Reine. "Why, I thought I recognized you. Aren't you Julian and Bernadette Jonson's granddaughter?"

"Yes, I am, Mrs. Saunders. It's nice to see you again."

The housekeeper smiled. "You gave me quite a start, dear. Sitting there in that rocker with little Sarah in your arms, you're the image of your mother." She shook her head. "That long dark hair and those big brown eyes and delicate features. Jacqueline used to sit in the rocker on the front porch at your grandparents' house and rock you and your brother for hours when you were children."

Reine nodded. "That was a long time ago."

Jonah popped to his feet. "Did you say the pies were done, Mrs. Saunders? Is it too close to dinner for us to have some?"

The housekeeper narrowed her eyes at the little boy. "I don't suppose a small piece would hurt your unbelievable appetite, as long as you don't bring any slithering, cold-blooded creatures into the kitchen. I'll have no snakes crawling around my work space."

Jonah glanced with obvious caution at his uncle. "It was my fault, Uncle Stephen. Please don't punish Peter."

"We'll discuss fault and punishment later." Stephen Morley reached out and set a hand on the little boy's shoulder. "Go and have your pie, Jonah."

"Me too?" Peter rose and stood beside his brother.

"You too." Stephen turned to Reine and leaned down to lift his niece into his arms. "Would you mind showing Miss Jonson to the study on your way to the kitchen, Mrs. Saunders? I'll just take Sarah up to the nursery."

He settled the little girl against his broad shoulder and held out his hand to Reine. "Miss Jonson?"

She looked at his outstretched hand and realized that he was offering to help her to her feet. Setting her fingers against his palm, she stood up from the rocker.

His grasp was steady and gentle before he released his hold. No smile brightened his handsome face, but she was surprised by the warmth his hand left on her fingertips. She liked the way her hand had fit into his, but she tried to ignore the little flutter of her heart as he strode from the room with his niece in his arms. Perhaps he liked plain vanilla ice cream just like she did, but that didn't mean anything, right?

Chapter Four

Reine was still thinking about Stephen's brief touch on her skin when Peter and Jonah led her halfway down the hall. Peter opened an oak door with a brass knob.

"Sit down anywhere." Jonah swept his hand toward the bright sunlit room with French doors leading to a garden full of colorful perennials and edged with evergreen shrubs. The scene appeared charming but somehow out of place in the craggy, weather-worn setting on the edge of Roanoke Sound. "Except in the chair behind the desk. That's where Uncle Stephen works."

Mrs. Saunders and the boys had not been gone long before Reine heard footsteps in the hall. Sitting in the comfortable, wing-backed chair near one corner of the large polished desk, she looked up to see Stephen Morley standing in the doorway.

"Miss Jonson, thank you for waiting. Again, I apologize for imposing on you and for subjecting you to a rather embarrassing and awkward situation. I hope I haven't kept you from other obligations."

She rose from her seat. "No, I have no plans until six-thirty, when my grandparents are expecting me to be at their house for dinner."

"Please sit." He rounded the desk corner and took a seat in the leather chair behind it. "May I get you something to drink? Lemonade? Iced tea? Coffee?"

"No, thank you." She clasped her hands on her lap. Her stomach twisted with nervousness and curiosity.

What do you want? She wished he would get to the point of the meeting.

He leveled intense, dark eyes on her. "You managed the children quite well."

The children? His remark caught her off guard, and she swallowed. Certainly he had not called her about the children.

"My nephews and niece seem to relate rather comfortably to you."

She shook her head. "Not me. Their favorite picture book. They really like that puppy story."

"And Sarah?"

"She definitely enjoys rocking."

He leaned back in his chair. "Do you have childcare experience?"

Again his question confused her. "Not really. I've done babysitting for some of the local residents, and I help with story hour at the library from time to time, but that's it."

He narrowed his eyes and set his hands on his desk. "I think your humility is misplaced, Miss Jonson. You should acknowledge your natural abilities."

Reine felt a blush rise up and heat her cheeks. "I wasn't being humble, just honest and realistic."

She wondered what natural abilities Stephen Morley had. It was obvious that he had a mind for business. Morley Cove Resort was thriving. In the three years since he had returned to Nags Head to manage the place, it had become one of the most popular tourist attractions in the area.

On the other hand, he often appeared to be unhappy. From her seat, she watched a shadow cross his angled face and could not help being curious about what kind of sadness filled his thoughts. Once again, she wondered if he ever smiled.

He sighed. "It is quite refreshing to see such a sense of realism in one so young."

Reine felt her cheeks burn, and she swallowed a retort. "I'm twenty-seven, Mr. Morley."

He raised his eyebrows. "It was not my intention to offend you."

A knock on the open door surprised Reine, and she turned to see Jonah grinning at her. The little blond boy bounced in the doorway as he clapped his hands.

"I'm not interrupting, am I, Reine? Mrs. Saunders said I shouldn't bother you, but I wanted to come and see if you and Uncle Stephen would like some pie. And some coffee." He licked his lips. "It's delicious. The pie, I mean. I had milk with mine. Do you want some?"

Reine shook her head. "No, thank you, Jonah. I'm having dinner in a little while, and I'm afraid a snack would spoil my appetite."

Jonah shrugged his small shoulders. "Nothing spoils my appetite. I'm always hungry." He turned to his uncle behind the desk. "You're not afraid of ruining your dinner, are you, Uncle Stephen? Do you want some blueberry pie?"

"Is there vanilla ice cream to go with it?"

Vanilla ice cream? Deborah's theory regarding ice cream flavors and relationships crossed her mind.

"Mrs. Saunders got chocolate ripple at the store when she went shopping."

Reine watched Stephen Morley frown. *And you don't like chocolate ripple?*

"I'll have a piece of pie without any ice cream after my

meeting with Miss Jonson. Thank you, Jonah. Now, leave and let us finish our discussion."

"I want to stay." The little boy sent a pleading look in Reine's direction. "Will you read the penguin story to me after you're done talking to Uncle Stephen?"

"Jonah Morley."

The child hung his head. "Yes, sir. I'm leaving."

When Reine turned back to the little boy's uncle, she was startled to find him looking at her. She smiled. "What a sweet child."

"Sweet? He put a grass snake on his nanny's tea tray and scared her into quitting. He's a little monster."

She could not tell for sure if his words were serious or teasing ones. "He's insisting that he was trying to keep his pet warm. I believe it was an innocent mistake."

"Aside from the fact that a snake does not constitute a house pet, Jonah's *innocent* mistake puts me in the very difficult position of finding someone to replace Miss Eddleton. It's not practical for me to take much time off work during the summer season. The resort is far too busy."

"Can't the children's parents take care of them?" She asked the question before she realized how impertinent it sounded. It was none of her business why Stephen Morley's niece and nephews were staying at his home.

From across the desk, he lowered his eyes and stared at the surface of the empty blotter in front of him. Deep lines etched his forehead. His expression made him appear unhappy and vulnerable.

Reine watched him as compassion filled her heart. Stephen Morley was rich and powerful and successful. Authoritative people like him were usually in command of any situation. They needed no one. At least, that was what she had always thought.

When he looked up at her again, his dark eyes were full of unexpressed sorrow. "They're dead. My brother Guy, who was five years younger than I, and his wife, Samantha, were killed in a climbing accident in Europe two weeks ago."

"Those three adorable little children are orphans?"

He nodded. "I am now their legal guardian."

That's why you had to resign from the community choir and why Mrs. Saunders bought unusual grocery items at the market. You have three children to care for now.

Reine cleared her throat as tears misted her eyes. "I'm very sorry for your loss, Mr. Morley. How sad for all of you."

His eyes held hers with a power she could not explain. In his own sorrow, he seemed to be analyzing her feelings. Could he read her thoughts? At the moment, in the bright, comfortable study at the Morley beach house, she imagined he could.

He squared his shoulders. "I'm afraid we've somehow strayed from the topic of our meeting."

She inhaled a deep breath. "What exactly is that, Mr. Morley? I'm not sure I understand why you asked me here this afternoon."

Nodding again, he sat forward in his chair. "The planning committee for the upcoming Summer Fun Days has asked me to head the festivities this year."

She brushed a few stray tears from her eyes as she tried to focus on the change in subject. Her thoughts continued to return to the three little children who had just lost their parents. "That's quite an honor, Mr. Morley. Of course, it makes sense that you take a prominent role in the celebration. After all, the Morley family settled in Nags Head years ago. I understand that your ancestors were some of the first permanent residents of the area."

"So I've heard."

"You don't believe they were?"

"I am a skeptic by nature, Miss Jonson."

She slid to the edge of her chair. "Okay, then. Forget your ancestry. You are a successful member of the community today in your own right. Regardless of your family's history, you deserve to join in the festivities."

A strand of thick, dark hair fell across the worry lines along his forehead. "You present a good argument and offer encouragement at the same time. I am beginning to understand why the children find your presence so comforting."

He shifted in his chair. "Nonetheless, Miss Jonson, I am enlisting your help. The reason I asked you here today is that all of this talk of family and ancestry has piqued my interest in my family's involvement in the settlement of the Outer Banks." He leveled his dark eyes on her questioning ones. "Everyone I have asked says that you are the genealogical research expert in the barrier islands area."

"I'm hardly an expert, Mr. Morley. I do historical research for local residents as part of my job at the library, and I also work on private requests to study documents and to write reports regarding specific aspects of individual family histories."

He lifted his brows above dark eyes. "Still humble, Miss Jonson?"

She squared her shoulders. "I've never claimed to be an authority on the study of family lineage."

"Nevertheless, you know much more about the subject than I do, and I'd like to hire you."

"Hire me for what, Mr. Morley?"

"To gather and summarize significant details on the settling of this area and the history of the Morley family so I am able to appear somewhat knowledgeable at the opening ceremonies of the Summer Fun Days next month. Is that in the realm of your expertise?"

She was not sure if he was teasing her, but she nodded. "Of course."

"Tell me about your credentials. Why are you qualified to do such work?"

"I have a bachelor's degree from the University of North Carolina, where I majored in history and political science. My plan is to take graduate courses in local history and anthropology, but I'm still trying to save money for classes."

"I see. Will it be possible for you to collect some interesting facts about the Outer Banks for me within the next week?"

Reine swallowed and tried to ignore the pull of his gaze on her. Those dark eyes seemed to perceive and to analyze her silent hesitation.

Researching historical facts was something she enjoyed, but delving into the personal details of Stephen Morley's life and family made her uncomfortable. Unlike Deborah, Reine had no interest in investigating the hidden secrets of the prominent businessman's ancestors.

She inhaled another deep breath. "I will compile a history of the area for you by the end of next week."

He leaned forward in his chair. "What is your usual fee?"

She shook her head. "The library will gratefully accept a small donation in return for the report, but you will not be charged. Providing research about the area is part of my responsibilities there."

"That's not a very wise way to run a business."

"Not every organization is concerned about making a profit."

"It's the old furniture issue, isn't it?"

Reine was completely confused again. "Furniture?"

"You're looking for furniture to sell to raise funds for the children's library, not the money itself. You work for the community center to provide a service to the public, but you don't want to be paid what you're worth for the job that you do."

"I receive a fair salary."

"I doubt that." He leveled his eyes on her from across the desk. "If I wanted, could I hire you as a private consultant to compile research on the Morley family? To write a genealogical report? I would be allowed to pay you then, right?"

Reine squared her shoulders. "I'm afraid I'm too busy right now to begin such a large research project, Mr. Morley."

"I wonder if there is another reason you do not want to accept my offer."

She stared at him. "I am in the middle of several other projects at the moment."

"So you would take the assignment at another time, then?"

"Perhaps. You are very persistent, Mr. Morley."

"And you, Miss Jonson, are very obstinate. You remind me of someone."

Obstinate? She had used the same word to describe him on Sunday.

Before she had a chance to comment, he snapped his fingers. "Niles Jonson, of course. You are related to him, I suppose?"

In spite of her irritation, she smiled. "My brother."

Stephen Morley nodded. "Yes, he is also resolute in his ideas."

"Don't you mean *obstinate*?"

For a moment, she thought she had gone too far. After all, the poor man was grieving for his brother and sister-in-law.

She watched him rise from his chair. "Well, I should not take up any more of your time. Perhaps in the future you may agree to do a detailed genealogy of the Morley family. At that time, I will insist on compensating you fairly for such a challenging task. In the meantime, will you compile some historical information for me to use during the Summer Fun Days?"

She stood up from her seat on the other side of the imposing desk. "Yes, I promise to have a completed report for you within a week, Mr. Morley."

He shook the hand she held out to him. "It's Stephen, Miss Jonson."

"Stephen." His first name sounded pleasant to her ears. She

retrieved her canvas bag from the floor next to her seat. "You can call me Reine. I'll notify your office when I've finished your research."

"Thank you, Reine. I look forward to seeing you again soon."

Stephen stood in the hall of his house and watched Reine Jonson walk a bicycle along the gravel drive toward Morley Cove Road. She did not run but hurried in a manner that made him wonder if he had kept her from another pressing appointment. Her feet seemed to glide with grace and ease in her low-heeled shoes as she reached the pavement, climbed onto the bike, and disappeared from his sight around a curve.

Who was she? Who was the quiet, unassuming woman who appeared on his doorstep at the precise moment that his life seemed to be falling apart around him?

Of course, he had seen her at choir concerts and other community events around the village, but Sunday was the first time he had really noticed her. She had been so adamant about not accepting his monetary donation. He had seen her again at the little ice cream shop in the village. Strands of her long, thick hair had been spilling over the shoulders of her smudged and wrinkled T-shirt; and, despite his fondness for neatness, he could not help but find her look appealing. *Why?*

Reine Jonson. When he had asked members of his staff to find someone knowledgeable about the history of the village, many had returned to him with the same name. *Reine Jonson.*

He shook his head as he closed the front door. It was probably good that she had turned down his proposal to write the Morley genealogy. She was a stubborn woman with strong principles that would, more than likely, end up clashing with his own ideas about the project.

He headed toward the kitchen feeling unsettled and irritable.

If it were, in fact, good that she had turned down his offer, why then did he feel so dissatisfied with the outcome of their meeting?

Reine sat down to the kitchen table with her grandparents and brother and poured ice water into each of their glasses. She smiled at her grandfather as she took the bowl of stew from him.

"You look tired, chickadee. You shouldn't work so late."

"I wasn't working exactly. I went over to Morley Cove Road after I finished at the library this afternoon to meet with Stephen Morley."

Niles looked up from the newspaper he was reading. "What's this I hear? You went to his house?"

Niles' grandmother placed a hand on his shoulder. "Put that paper down while we're eating."

Reine's grandfather turned back to her. "Young Stephen is starting to become very prominent in the community, isn't he?"

Niles folded the paper and set it beside his plate. "Young Stephen?"

"His father, also Stephen Morley, used to charter a boat, and hired me as his guide to take him and his young sons Gulf Stream fishing once a year when he came down from New York to check on the management at the resort. It was called Morley Inn then."

Her grandfather paused as he took a bite of stew and swallowed. "Morley was very strict with those boys. Fishing should be fun, but that man was all business, even when he was trying to teach his sons to fish." Julian Jonson shook his head. "He demanded perfection in everything those boys did. He had rules for baiting the hooks, holding the poles, and reeling in the lines. It wasn't hard to see that his sons couldn't wait to get off the boat at the end of the day."

"Why, that's just awful." Reine's grandmother passed the salad bowl to Julian. "I wonder if Stephen and his brother ever learned to enjoy fishing."

Niles chuckled. "I think Stephen despises the sport. He practically cringes whenever he has to discuss the subject with me."

"Ah, yes." Reine's grandfather passed a basket of rolls to Reine. "You've been doing weekend runs for some of Morley's guests."

Niles nodded. "I offered to take him out with me one day, but he flatly refused."

Bernadette buttered a roll. "So young Stephen and his brother never fish?"

"Guy." Reine added tossed salad to her plate. "Stephen's brother's name is . . . was Guy. He died two weeks ago."

The older woman stared at her. "He did? What a tragedy."

Niles raised his eyebrows. "I think he was around your age, Reine. Morley's mentioned his brother a couple of times. He lived in New York, didn't he?"

"I don't know. Both he and his wife were killed in Europe. They left behind three children."

Bernadette shook her head. "There was nothing in the paper about that. I wonder if we should send a condolence card to Stephen. He must be devastated."

Reine's grandfather nodded. "His father died of a heart attack over ten, no, twelve years ago."

"I haven't heard anything about Mrs. Morley in years. I wonder whatever happened to her."

Reine shrugged. "He didn't mention his mother, but Guy's children are staying with Stephen at his house on Morley Cove Road."

"You seem to be quite familiar with his personal life, chickadee."

"Yes, I find it interesting that Stephen Morley should share so much with you, dear," her grandmother said. "If I remember correctly, the members of that family have always been very private people who keep mostly to themselves."

Her grandfather nodded. "It surprises me that young Stephen has agreed to play such a major role in the Summer Fun Days. The Morleys never really seemed to fit in as local residents or as tourists. As your grandmother said, they are very reserved people."

Niles chuckled again. "He told me he's not at all thrilled about being asked to head the events."

Reine nodded. "He's not. He wants me to do some research about the history of the Outer Banks." She did not add that she had declined his adamant request to work on a genealogy of the Morley family. As she took a drink of ice water, she recalled the hysterical scene she had witnessed as she arrived at the beach house earlier that afternoon. "He just happened to mention his brother's death."

Her grandfather smiled. "You're a good listener, chickadee. Stephen could probably use a trusting friend right now."

A trusting friend. Reine had difficulty imagining being friends with someone who never smiled. She wondered if she and Stephen Morley shared a single common interest, aside from the fact that they both preferred vanilla ice cream.

"Hold on, Reine." Niles hurried toward her across their grandparents' gravel driveway. He fell into step beside her on the sidewalk lined with old, wind-blown pines.

A cricket chirped nearby in the evening heat.

"I can give you a ride home, you know."

"It's only half a mile to my apartment."

"I ran into Don Jenkins today at the pier. He was delivering a truck he had just repaired. He told me about your car."

Reine sighed. "It needs a lot of work."

"He told me you'd be better off financing another one. I agree with him."

"Well, I don't have the money right now."

"My offer still stands, Reine. An interest-free loan for as long as you need it."

"And my answer still stands. Thanks, but no."

"You're just being obstinate."

That was the second time during the evening someone had used that word to describe her. It was starting to become annoying.

She stopped on the sidewalk and looked up at her brother. "I appreciate what you're trying to do, Niles, but I don't want to be responsible for a big loan right now. I want to pay off my undergraduate loans and go to graduate school part-time. My plan does not include begging my brother for money."

"You're not begging. I'm offering. Consider it an investment in your future."

She started to walk again. "Why? So I'll take care of you when you retire?"

Niles chuckled. "I'm not sure my wife would want you to do that."

"Your wife? You're not even dating anyone, are you?"

"That doesn't mean I don't plan to find my true love and marry her one day. You might want to consider that possibility for yourself, as well."

"You're beginning to sound like Deborah."

"It's been over a year since you and Alan broke up. He's not worth pining over."

"I'm not pining."

"Then get on with your life. Go out and meet someone."

She sighed. "I don't know. I feel more comfortable researching other people's family trees than considering the future of my own."

"You don't want to spend the rest of your life alone, do you?"

"Maybe not. I don't know. I just haven't met anyone, I guess."

"While we're on the subject—"

"What subject?"

"Dating."

"I'm not interested, Niles. I don't have time to date right now."

"I know, but you can take a night off from writing the genealogies of every person in North Carolina."

"I took last night off."

"Yeah, right. To collect donations for the community center. I mean an actual night off. Listen, Reine, I need a date for Saturday night. I'd really appreciate your company."

"What's going on?"

"There's an Outer Banks Business Association dinner dance that I should attend, but I don't want to go by myself. It's always awkward going to these social events alone."

"You should talk to Deb. I'm sure she could set you up with someone."

He laughed. "She's given me a couple of suggestions. Anyway, will you come with me? It's a casual affair, so you don't even have to dress up much, and I promise we won't stay late."

"Oh, all right. Where is it?"

"Thanks, Reine. I'll pick you up at six-thirty. The dinner is in the Pelican Room in the main lodge of Morley Cove Resort."

Chapter Five

Reine did not sleep well at all that night. For some reason she could not explain, Stephen Morley's handsome, unsmiling face drifted in and out of her thoughts. His dark, probing eyes and quiet voice teased her unconscious in an endless series of meetings with him at his beach house, in his office at Morley Cove Resort, and even at her own place of employment. In every scene, he asked her to research a different branch of his family tree.

When she realized that she would get no restful sleep, she rose early from her sofa bed, showered, and dressed for the day. She spent the next few hours before work taking notes on the history of the village and the settlement of the Morley family. Although her findings were interesting, the task did not take her mind off the aloof, unhappy man who lived with his young niece and nephews on the shore of Roanoke Sound. Finally, she filled a travel mug with coffee and headed for the Nags Head Library and Community Center on foot.

Alone in her office, she organized her notes and then typed up on her desktop computer the report Stephen Morley had requested. She sipped her coffee as she proofread the information she had compiled and made a few edits. Then she printed the report and filed one copy in the cabinet in the storage room before slipping another copy into a large manila envelope to deliver to Stephen's office at Morley Cove Resort.

She thought that by completing the work, she would be able to concentrate on something besides his dark, sad eyes, but she was wrong. She began to wonder if she should tell Niles that she could not attend the dinner with him on Saturday at the resort.

At five o'clock Friday afternoon, Reine walked to Ocean-front Market to pick up Deborah's car. It was filled with donations she and Jeremy had collected the previous evening, and Reine had offered to unload everything into the storage garage at the community center after she dropped off Stephen Morley's report at his office.

"Thanks a lot, Reine. Jeremy and I are going to a beach concert in Kitty Hawk, so I don't have time to unload all the stuff tonight. The whole backseat is full of computer monitors and towers. I put the keyboards and other accessories on the floorboards. I'll pick up the car at your apartment sometime tomorrow."

Reine pulled out of the parking area at the market into the heavy summer afternoon traffic. Pedestrians were everywhere, so she had to reduce her speed until she turned off onto Morley Cove Road. Turning left instead of right toward the beach house, she drove the remaining mile to a shady parking area at one end of the main lodge of Morley Cove Resort. There she was met by a young man in khaki pants and a dark green polo shirt with the resort emblem of an egret and a sailboat embroidered on the pocket.

After assuring the valet that she was able to park her car without assistance, she selected a place shaded by loblolly pine branches from a grove of weathered evergreens, where picnic tables and stone fireplaces had been set along a nature walk leading to a private beach at the edge of Morley Cove in Roanoke Sound.

Despite the fact that the pine tree branches shaded her car from the direct late-afternoon sun, Reine rolled down both passenger- and driver-side windows before she picked up her canvas bag from the other seat. She did not want the computer components to be damaged by the heat.

Taking a deep breath to calm her nerves, she looked up at the main lodge and center of activity at Morley Cove Resort. The structure was a three-story building in the design of an over-sized Swiss chalet, with numerous balconies and railings edged with colorful potted annual flowers. From where Reine stood in the parking area, she could see several stone paths leading from the lodge to small and large cottages that could accommodate groups of guests or individual families, according to information Reine had read in advertisements and brochures.

"Hey, Reine! Is it really you?"

She scanned the front of the lodge to find the source of the voice calling her. From a wide balcony on the second floor, she saw a little boy waving his arms.

"Hi, Jonah."

"Are you coming up? I have the puppy book."

Before she had time to answer, a tall young man in khaki pants and a green polo shirt picked up the child and disappeared through a set of wood-framed glass doors.

Reine tossed her car keys into her canvas bag and slid the straps onto her shoulder. Heading toward the main entrance, she ascended steps to a wide porch with wicker furniture and deck chairs painted in earth tones. Guests sitting with colorful fruit drinks smiled and nodded to her as she reached the doors.

Everyone seemed happy and friendly. Reine wondered if

the people who stayed at Morley Cove Resort were always so content. Although she had lived her whole life in Nags Head, she had visited the private beach for picnics only a few times and had never been an overnight guest at the lodge or in one of the cottages.

The large open lobby with unlit fireplaces on each end and comfortable-looking sofas and chairs arranged in clusters around the polished hardwood floor provided an atmosphere of hospitality and comfort. Reine scanned the area with keen interest as she approached what appeared to be the main desk.

"May I help you?" A young woman in khaki slacks and green polo shirt smiled at her.

"I have some papers for Mr. Morley. I called earlier to tell his secretary that I'd be stopping by with them."

The resort employee nodded and picked up the phone on the high desk between them. She spoke for a few moments and then replaced the receiver.

"If you don't mind waiting, Mr. Morley will be back from his meeting shortly."

"I understand that Mr. Morley's nephews are here."

"Oh, you know the children? Yes, they've been around most of the day. Right now, one of the recreation staff members is keeping the boys entertained, I think. Mr. Morley's assistant has the little girl with her."

"His assistant?"

"Gwyneth Coulter. Her office is next to his on the second floor. Would you like to go up there and see the children while you wait?"

"Sure. How do I get there?"

After obtaining directions from the cheerful resort employee at the desk, Reine ascended the wide wooden stairs with railings on both sides entwined with strings of tiny white lights that made her think of fairy tales and castles. Before she reached the door labeled *Management*, she heard a child's cry and an adult calling out in a loud voice.

When no one answered her knock, she turned the knob and entered a small reception area. The telephone on the desk in front of an empty chair was ringing, and several doors leading from the room were ajar. The unhappy cries of a child pierced the air, and words of obvious frustration from an adult female accompanied the noise.

As Reine stood by the desk trying to decide what she should do next, a tall, thin man in the familiar khaki and green uniform stepped into the reception area. He rushed to answer the telephone just as it stopped ringing.

At the same moment, Jonah darted into the room. Another staff member, one with red hair and freckles, followed him.

A wide smile brightened the child's face for a moment. "Reine, I'm so glad you're here. Tell Robbie to give me the puppy book." Jonah clutched her hand and tipped his head to look up at her. His big blue eyes glistened with unshed tears. "He won't let me have it."

"We read it five times already, champ. Let's do something else."

Reine watched the little boy shake his blond head at the staff member who had followed him into the reception room. The crying child's wails increased in volume.

She turned as a young, slender woman with short dark hair and a pinched expression on her face stepped through one of the open doorways. In a slim-fitting dark suit and lacy white blouse, she struggled to hold onto Sarah, who squirmed and kicked with simultaneous movements.

Reine held her breath when the woman attempted to keep herself balanced on wobbling stiletto heels as the little girl struggled to get free. She imagined that any second the two would fall into a pile on the hardwood floor of the reception area. The telephone rang again.

"This child screams all the time."

Jonah tightened his hold on Reine's hand. "Sarah needs a nap."

Reine nodded as she recalled how the child had fallen asleep in her arms the previous day. She cleared her throat. When she spoke, she was forced to increase her volume until she could be heard above Sarah's cries. "Jonah may be right. Sarah could be tired."

The slender woman balancing on high heels glared at Reine. "And who are you?"

"This is Reine, and my sister likes her." Jonah squeezed her hand. "Let Reine hold Sarah."

"Come on, champ. We have to go find your brother." The red-haired staff member tried to take Jonah's hand. "Where did he run off to, anyway?"

Jonah clung to Reine's arm. "No, I want to stay here."

Reine watched the other uniformed man's shoulders slump. "I'll read the puppy book again if you help me find your brother."

She felt a rush of concern wash over her as she looked down at Jonah. "You can't find Peter? Where do you think he went?"

The telephone rang again. The staff member at the desk answered as though nothing unusual was happening around him.

Jonah's expression was solemn. "He went to find Uncle Stephen because Sarah doesn't like Gwyneth. She just cries and cries. You'd better take her."

Reine glanced at the woman struggling with the little girl. It was obvious that Stephen Morley's assistant was upset about the situation. She was brushing strands of dark hair from her flushed face as her blue eyes darted to Reine.

Reine forced a smile at Jonah. "Why don't you go with . . . ?"

"Robbie Moreland," the young man said as his freckled cheeks turned bright red.

Reine squatted in front of the little boy. "Why don't you go with Robbie and help him find Peter? He says he'll read the puppy story to you again."

Finally Jonah released his tight grip on her arm. A slight smile replaced the serious expression on his little face. "Robbie put it on a high shelf in the playroom."

"Let's go get it, champ." Robbie held out a hand to the child. "We'll take it along while we look for your big brother. Maybe we can read it down at the beach."

Reine gave Jonah's shoulder a gentle squeeze and nodded. "Go ahead."

The little boy took Robbie's hand. With a small sigh of relief, Reine turned to face the frustrated woman holding Sarah.

"She likes to rock. Do you have a rocking chair around here?"

"What? I can't hear you above this screaming."

Reine held out her arms. "May I try taking her?"

Stephen Morley's assistant stared at her for a long moment and then shrugged. "I'm really sick of watching her. Babysitting is *not* part of my job description."

She shoved the squirming child into Reine's outstretched arms. "What did you say your name was again?"

"It's Reine Jonson." She rubbed Sarah's back. "I'm the director of the local library and community center."

"Oh, Miss Jonson, yes." The tall, thin man answering the telephone walked toward her from behind the desk. "We've been expecting you."

He patted Sarah's curly head. "That's the quietest she's been all day. Jonah's right. She likes you."

"She doesn't like anybody. She's just tired herself out." Gwyneth frowned. "Reine Jonson? I don't think I recognize the name."

"I'm Mr. Morley's secretary." The young man held out his hand to Reine. "My name is Terry Deacon. This is Gwyneth Coulter, Mr. Morley's executive assistant."

With care, Reine removed her right arm from around Sarah and shook Terry's hand. "I have the research notes for Mr. Morley."

Gwyneth continued to frown at her. "What kind of research? I certainly hope Stephen is having you research perspective applicants for a nanny position."

Reine tightened her hold on Sarah as the child whimpered. "No, just some historical information for the village's Summer Fun Days next month."

"Here, let me show you to the playroom. There's a rocking chair in there." Terry led her through the doorway from which everyone had entered the reception area and into a large bright, cheery room with low, white-painted chairs and tables just the right size for young children.

Bay windows overlooked the smooth water of Morley Cove, and the window seats were piled with colorful cushions. Toys, board games, easels, and art supplies covered shelves along two walls. A pair of white wicker rockers stood next to a large bookcase of children's books.

"This is the nursery the children of resort employees use for occasional daycare. We have a much larger one on the first floor that is open every day for the guests."

Terry smiled again as a phone began to ring. "Go ahead. Use the rocking chairs or anything else you need, Miss Jonson. I'll tell Mr. Morley you're in here."

Carrying his briefcase and a pile of manila file folders, Stephen rounded the corner of the corridor and headed toward his office. With impatience, he ran his free hand through his hair. *What a day!*

First the temporary babysitter quit, and he had to find staff members to watch three upset children. Then he missed lunch because of a mix-up in supply deliveries. Later, his afternoon meeting ran over by an hour and was interrupted by Peter reporting about how unhappy Sarah was with his executive assistant.

He sighed as he approached the nursery. The door was ajar, but there were no sounds of activity coming from the room.

He reached for the knob and began to close the door, but a movement caught his eye. Someone was sitting in one of the rocking chairs at the far end of the room.

He blinked and thought he must be mistaken. Motionless, he stood in the doorway and watched the quiet scene before him.

Strands of dark shoulder-length hair fell across Reine Jonson's pale cheek as she moved her feet to keep the rocker in motion while she hummed a soft tune. Either asleep or very still, his niece lay against Reine's shoulder as one tiny little hand clutched the knit fabric of the young woman's pale yellow sleeveless sweater.

He cleared his throat and must have startled Reine, because she stopped rocking and turned her head toward him. Sarah whimpered and squirmed in her arms.

"Stay there." He whispered the words as he held up the palm of his free hand to stop her. "Don't get up."

A slight flush colored her cheeks as she pushed against the floor to put the rocker back in motion. She patted Sarah until the little girl snuggled against her shoulder again.

Stephen set his briefcase and folders on a nearby table and crossed to the other rocking chair. "What are you doing here?" He kept his voice low as he took a seat beside her.

He reached out to finger one of his niece's soft blonde curls. Sarah sighed and hugged Reine.

"I came by to drop off the historical research I did for you."

Even as she whispered, her words had a certain serene quality. He realized he liked to listen to her speak. Her voice had a soft, soothing quality.

"Already?" Her presence had a calming effect on him, just

as seeing her in the rocking chair holding Sarah seemed to settle his nerves.

He leaned back in his seat and began to rock. "This actually feels good. I don't think I've ever spent any time in one of these, at least not as an adult."

Reine looked at him with wide brown eyes. The bright afternoon sunlight streaming through the windows accented tiny gold flecks in her eyes that he had not noticed until that moment.

He stroked Sarah's soft curls again. "This little one certainly enjoys rocking."

"She was having a rough moment when I came up here to wait for you."

He lifted his eyebrows. "Rough *moment*? You do have a way of making understatements. According to my staff, Sarah hasn't stopped crying all day."

She rubbed the child's back. "She's had a lot of changes to deal with."

"She seems to have adjusted well to you."

Reine did not respond to his comment but continued to maintain a rhythm of gentle movement in the rocking chair. "Are the boys okay?"

He pulled his attention back to her question. The scene she created was so peaceful. He wished he had time to stay there and relax and not have to think about the problems that had complicated his day.

"Now they are. Mrs. Saunders called me at about ten this morning to tell me that the temporary babysitter I thought I had been fortunate enough to hire on such short notice had quit. Apparently, the young lady had dropped all three children back at home less than an hour after I took them to her house."

"An emergency?"

He frowned. "Yes, an invitation to go sailing. According to

Mrs. Saunders, the babysitter, the teenage daughter of one of my front desk managers, decided that she would rather spend the day at the beach with her friends than take care of three energetic children."

Reine's expression turned sad, and she hugged the child in her arms. "That's too bad. It's no wonder Peter, Jonah, and Sarah seem so unsettled. More than anything, they need some permanence in their lives right now, not more confusion."

"I know. I'm trying." He dragged a hand through his hair and ignored the thought that it probably matched his emotions, disheveled and confused. Would his life ever return to normal?

"I've checked every employment agency within one hundred miles. No one is looking for a nanny position. Even babysitters are difficult to find in the summer. The few private daycares have no vacancies for *three* children."

He shook his head. "I can't ask Mrs. Saunders to increase her hours to watch them. She works long enough cleaning the house and cooking for us. The resort staff daycare was designed for temporary supervision only, when unforeseen events occur in the lives of staff members that might keep them from working, not for permanent childcare situations. Anyway, I really would prefer to find someone who is willing to stay at the house with them."

"That would be the ideal solution. I'm sure Sarah and the boys are feeling distressed and unhappy right now. Your home is still new to them, and today they had to spend the day with strangers."

Stephen rocked in silence for a few moments. "So far, I haven't proven to be a very competent guardian, have I?"

Her large brown eyes appeared surprised. "Oh, no, I wasn't thinking that at all. I can't imagine how difficult it must be for you. Anyone would struggle in such a situation."

"Not you, it seems."

She shook her head. "I was just helping out, Mr. Morley."

"Stephen."

"Yes, Stephen." A blush colored her pale cheeks. "I should go."

She slowed the rocker with her feet and rose. His hand brushed hers as she placed the little girl against his shoulder.

Warmth from her fingers surprised him. Her compassion and serenity, combined with a smile that cheered him when he thought he could never feel happiness again, were remarkable. Reine Jonson was remarkable.

He watched her pull a large envelope from the canvas bag on the floor near the rocker, the bag she had carried with her to his house the previous afternoon. She set it a few feet away from them on a low table piled with sturdy wooden puzzles for children.

"I'll leave these notes for you to review. Let me know if you need any other information."

"That was fast. I didn't expect you to do the research so soon." He met her eyes. "I'd like to pay you for your time."

"No, thank you. I told you that doing historical research for local residents is part of my job. The library pays me an adequate salary."

"You're not riding your bike again today, are you?"

She shook her head, and strands of thick, brown hair slid back and forth across her shoulders. In her yellow sleeveless sweater, beige slacks, and leather sandals, she looked like she was ready to go on a picnic at the beach or a boat ride in the cove. He wondered where Reine Jonson was going that evening and with whom she was spending her free time.

"No, I have a car today. Goodbye, Stephen."

Long after Reine had left the playroom, Stephen sat holding Sarah and thinking about her. Despite the numerous demands of his day and his typical ability to keep focused, he had found his mind drifting often to the intriguing young woman who seemed to have materialized out of nowhere and was now appearing everywhere he went. Her brown eyes were full of expression, and her smile was unforgettable. Reine Jonson had the loveliest smile he had ever seen.

Shaking his head, he rose from the rocking chair. He held Sarah with one arm as he retrieved Reine's envelope, the pile of file folders, and his briefcase before crossing the floor of the nursery. He still had work to do, and he had no idea how he would do it with a small child sleeping against his shoulder.

Reine hurried to Deborah's car in the main parking area of Morley Cove Resort and slid behind the steering wheel. As she pulled into traffic on the main street, the image of Stephen holding his little niece flashed through her mind. He had looked so tired and frustrated. In fact, he had seemed more upset and disillusioned about his life's circumstances than she was about her own, even with the financial difficulties she was experiencing at the moment. Being rich and influential certainly did not appear to make the problems in Stephen's world any easier for him.

She pulled into the driveway of the old wind-worn house where she rented an apartment on the second floor. Examining the clear blue sky, she debated about whether or not to close the back windows of Deb's car. There was no rain in the forecast, and she planned to unload the car as soon as she changed out of her work clothes.

Slipping her canvas bag over her shoulder, she headed up the sand-covered walk to the steps leading up a full floor to the wide porch on the second story of the structure. The two old rocking chairs with faded nautical-print cushions reminded Reine again of the Morley children and their handsome, aloof uncle who never smiled.

Her heart felt heavy, and she realized that she was sad for them. As she unlocked the door and stepped into her apartment, Reine heard her telephone ringing. Tossing her bag onto a nearby chair, she rushed through her tiny living room to her even smaller galley kitchen and lifted the receiver from the wall unit.

"Reine? I'm so glad you're home. It's Stephen Morley."

Astonished by the identity of the caller and the urgency in his voice, Reine swallowed and struggled to hold the phone with a shaking hand. Something was wrong.

"I just walked in. What is it?"

"Is Jonah with you?"

Her throat felt tight. "Jonah? No, of course not. Why?"

"He's missing, Reine. We can't find him anywhere."

"Missing?" She realized she was repeating Stephen's words as though he was speaking a foreign language, but she was stunned.

"One of my staff thinks he heard Jonah mention going to find you, probably about the same time that you left here. Apparently he said something about that picture book he likes so much." Stephen sighed. "No one took the child seriously. He's only five."

Only five and sad about losing his parents and his home. And now he's missing.

"Have you called the police?"

"Not yet. We've been searching everywhere here. I was going to notify the sheriff next, but I wanted to check with you first, just in case."

Reine's chest tightened as she heard the despair in the man's voice. She cleared her throat. "You'll find him, Stephen. What can I do to help?"

The pause before he spoke was long enough to cause her to think that Stephen had hung up the phone. A chill swept over her.

"Peter's very upset. I think he blames himself for not keeping a closer eye on Jonah. And Sarah, well, she's no longer sleeping."

"You need to call the sheriff and report that Jonah's missing. I'll come and stay with Peter and Sarah until you find him. Are you still at your office?"

"Yes." His voice was low and unsteady. "Thank you, Reine."

She replaced the receiver and pulled her car keys from her bag before hurrying back out into the hot, humid evening and down the stairs. As she slid behind the steering wheel of Deborah's car, a rustling sound behind her caught her attention.

She put the key into the ignition but did not start the car. Instead, she listened again. What was that noise?

For a moment, she thought that she was simply imagining things because she was so upset about Jonah's disappearance, but when she heard the sounds of movement a third time, she knew the noise was real. It seemed to be coming from the backseat of her friend's car.

She turned around and leaned into the backseat. With a shaking hand, she pulled up the old worn blanket from the floorboard. "Oh!"

The exclamation escaped from her as she dropped the blanket on a stack of computer towers. Curled up on the floorboard was a blond-haired child. As she watched, he raised his head and yawned.

"Hi, Reine."

"Jonah! What are you doing in here?"

The small boy stretched his arms. "I guess I fell asleep while I was hiding."

Hurrying from the front seat, she opened the back door and reached out to help the child climb out of the car. She gave him a long hug, and he clung to her.

"Why were you hiding, honey?"

"I wanted you to read the puppy story." He pointed to the

picture book on a pile of blankets on the backseat. "You're the only one who reads it like Mom did."

Tears stung her eyes as she set Jonah on his feet and handed the book to him. "We have to call your Uncle Stephen right away, Jonah. He's very worried about you."

"But he's so busy. I didn't think he'd mind. Anyway, he still has Peter and Sarah."

Taking the key, she closed the car doors. Then she took Jonah's hand.

"We forgot Chester in the backseat."

"Chester? Your pet snake? He's with you?"

"I couldn't leave him with Robbie. He doesn't like snakes."

Deborah's not too thrilled about them either. Especially in her car.

She imagined the little reptile crawling around inside the donated computer equipment. "Where is Chester now?"

He pointed into the car. "Somewhere on the seat."

Fortunately, the snake had not ventured far. Reine found the small creature curled up next to a pile of keyboards.

"Here, you hold Chester." She placed the snake in Jonah's outstretched hand. "We'll find a nice shoebox for him. I'll carry your book."

Reaching for the child's free hand, she led him along the sand-covered walk to the set of steps leading to her apartment. "You shouldn't have run off without telling someone, Jonah."

The little boy climbed the stairs beside her to the second floor. "I told Robbie I was going to go with you. I squeezed in the back. You have a lot of stuff in there."

Reine led him into her apartment. "It wasn't nice of you to hide from Robbie."

The child's blue eyes glistened with tears as he stroked the reptile's tiny body. "He didn't like Chester. He didn't want to read the puppy book again."

She squeezed his thin shoulders. "I know, honey. You've had

a really tough day. Come on. Sit on the couch with Chester. I'm going to call your uncle to let him know you're here. After that, I'll get you some milk and a box for Chester, and then we'll read your puppy book."

Chapter Six

Jonah was leaning against Reine's arm as they sat looking at his picture book in her apartment when someone knocked. She left the puppy story with the little boy as she rose to answer the door.

Stephen Morley's tired, drawn face and sad eyes met hers. Worry etched deep lines across his forehead, and strands of his dark hair stuck out in every direction as though he had dragged his fingers through it numerous times since he had last combed it.

He looked past her into her apartment. Sarah bounced in his arms and reached for Reine while Peter stood, with his head drooping, a few steps behind his uncle.

Reine took the little girl from Stephen as Jonah jumped off the sofa and bounded toward them. While Stephen caught his younger nephew in a close embrace, Reine carried Sarah onto the porch and kneeled near the older boy.

"It's okay now, Peter. Everything is all right. Jonah's safe."

"But it's all my fault."

She touched his pale cheek with her free hand. "No, Peter. It's not your job to watch Jonah. You're just a little boy too."

"I'm his big brother. I'm the oldest, so I have to look out for Jonah and Sarah. We don't have anyone else anymore."

"You have your Uncle Stephen, and he loves you very much. It's his job to take care of you now."

Peter stared at her. "Are you sure? It's not my fault?"

She smiled and slipped her arm around his trembling shoulders. "I'm sure. Why don't you come in and have some milk?"

Sarah bounced in her arms. "Me too."

Reine led Peter into her apartment where Stephen and Jonah were sitting on her living room couch. The little boy appeared to be listening with intense concentration to his uncle. She watched Jonah nod his blond head.

"Yes, Uncle Stephen, I know. Reine already told me it was wrong to run and hide from Robbie and the other people at your work. She said I should talk about how I feel and tell people what I need. She said I won't always get everything I want, but I should try to help people to understand."

"She did, did she?" Stephen met her gaze.

The deep concern in his blue eyes had faded, but his expression was still somber. Reine could not find even a hint of a smile on his handsome face.

"She told me it wasn't nice to worry you and everyone who was trying to help."

"I thirsty." Sarah bounced against Reine. "Want milk."

Jonah nodded. "I'll have some more milk too. And I'm getting hungry."

Stephen rose to his full height and seemed like a human tower in the small apartment. "We have to go, children. We've imposed on Reine quite enough for one afternoon."

"I thirsty!" Sarah squirmed in Reine's arms.

"What does *imposed* mean, Uncle Stephen?"

"Reine has to finish the puppy story. She promised."

Stephen held up his hands as all three of the children spoke at once. "Mrs. Saunders is preparing dinner for us at home."

"Reine can come and eat with us." Jonah pulled on her arm. "You'll have dinner at our house, won't you, Reine? You can be our nanny and eat with us all the time. I want you to come and take care of us. That way, we won't *impose* you again."

"That's a good idea, Uncle Stephen." Peter nodded his head. "Look at how much Sarah likes her. You know how picky she is. She doesn't like many people."

"I like Reine." Sarah patted Reine's cheeks and grinned at her. "Milk, please."

Stephen met Reine's gaze again and raised his brows above questioning eyes. "It seems you're much better at understanding these children than I am. Do *you* have any suggestions?"

"No, except that you should probably feed them soon."

"Come with us, Reine." Jonah jumped up and down, clapping his hands. "Mrs. Saunders always makes extra food."

"Jonah." Stephen set a hand on the little boy's shoulder. "Slow down. Reine may have other plans for dinner."

Jonah tipped his head to look at her. "You don't, do you?"

Sarah bounced against her hip. "I want cookies. I want milk."

Reine could not hold back a laugh of pure delight. She nodded as happy tears spilled from her eyes.

Looking around the room at the expressions of surprise on the faces of the two little boys and their uncle, she wiped her cheeks with the back of her free hand. "You win. I'll have dinner with you, but first I want to stop by my grandparents' and then unload my friend's car." She turned to Stephen. "I have Deb's, and it's loaded with garage sale donations."

"Your grandparents?" Jonah grinned at her. "They can come to dinner too."

She shook her head as she handed Sarah to Stephen. "They're going to a barbecue at a neighbor's this evening."

"What about *your* plans?"

She smiled at Stephen. "I just have to drop off those donations. Why don't you take these hungry children home now?
I'll meet you there as soon as I'm done."

Jonah clasped her hand. "Promise?"

She smoothed his blond hair. "I promise."

An hour later, Peter and Jonah answered the front door of the
beach house on Morley Cove Road when Reine arrived a few
minutes before seven o'clock. They grinned, poked each other,
and then led her into the large formal dining room, where the
table had been set with elegant china, silver, and two crystal
vases of yellow day lilies.

"I gave everybody a napkin," Jonah said.

"And I poured the water," Peter added as a swinging door at
the far end of the room opened and Stephen entered.

Reine smiled at him and met his eyes. She was surprised
when her heart seemed to stop for a split second before it
resumed its normal beat.

She noticed that although he had combed his hair and removed his suit jacket, he still wore the crisp, white shirt, tie,
and dress pants that he had been wearing at his office. Sarah
bounced and squirmed in his arms.

The room became quiet, and Reine could not explain the
sensation of tingling anticipation that hummed around her.
She swallowed and pulled her attention back to the table with
its sparkling glassware and polished silver.

"Everything looks so pretty." Her voice sounded low and
breathless to her ears. She cleared her throat. "I hope you didn't
fuss just for me."

Jonah took her hand and led her to the place setting adjacent
to the one at the head of the large rectangular table. "Uncle
Stephen said we should use the good dishes for dinner because
it's such a special night."

"Yes." Peter pulled out a dark walnut chair with a seat of

burgundy velvet. "We even cut flowers from the garden." The oldest child grinned up at his uncle, who was struggling to put the uncooperative little girl in a wooden high chair across from them.

"We're celebrating because Jonah's not lost anymore."

"And because we have a new friend. Uncle Stephen says it's important that we share what we have with friends, so we're sharing our dinner with you, Reine."

The boy's uncle turned from securing the buckle around Sarah's tiny waist to look at Reine. Her heart skipped a beat as Stephen's intense dark eyes held hers. *So I'm a friend now?*

"Take your seats, boys."

His voice sounded odd. Reine tried not to spend too much time wondering why.

He pulled his eyes from her. "I'll go see if Mrs. Saunders needs some help."

Sarah struck the wooden tray of her high chair with her little palms as Peter and Jonah chattered about their adventures at the resort that day until Stephen returned to the dining room with the housekeeper. They set bowls of baked potatoes and green beans and a platter of marinated chicken breasts on the table.

"It's not a very fancy meal." Mrs. Saunders smoothed the front of her apron. "I wasn't really prepared for company."

Reine smiled as she accepted a plate of warm bread from the older woman. "Everything looks delicious. Thank you for having me on such short notice."

The housekeeper returned the smile and waved her hand in the air. "It's been a crazy day around here. One more at dinner isn't so bad, but next time I would appreciate a little warning that a dinner guest is coming."

With a contrite, almost sheepish expression on his handsome face, Stephen looked up from cutting green beans on Sarah's plate. "Next time I promise to not be so inconsiderate."

Next time? Reine wondered when the next time would be

that she'd be invited to share a meal with Stephen Morley and his family.

Seemingly satisfied with his apology, Mrs. Saunders nodded and headed toward the kitchen door. "I'd better go check on dessert."

"I hope next time is soon." Jonah spread butter on his bread, as well as on the tips of his fingers and across his wrist. "I like having Reine eat dinner with us. Doesn't she look nice at the table, Uncle Stephen?"

"Yes, she does." Stephen's response in his quiet, baritone voice unnerved her.

Peter nodded. "I think you should hire Reine to take care of us, Uncle Stephen. It would solve all of our problems."

She watched Stephen scoop baked potato out of the skin for Sarah and waited for him to respond to the little boy's comment. When it appeared that he had no intention of doing so, she smiled across the table at Peter. "I have a job, but I'm sure your uncle will find a nanny for you soon."

Peter shook his head. "Not one like you."

Beside her, Jonah bobbed his head up and down several times as he licked butter from his fingers. "You're just the one we need, Reine."

"I'm not a nanny, Jonah."

"You're a perfect nanny." Peter speared a piece of chicken with his fork. "We all like you. Plus, you're the only one who can get Sarah to settle down to sleep, *and* you're the best at reading the puppy on the farm story just the way Jonah likes it."

"You even like Chester."

"Chester?" From the head of the table, Stephen looked up and leveled his dark eyes on Jonah. "Chester the snake?"

The little boy hung his head. "Yes."

"I thought we agreed that you would let Chester go out in the garden."

Jonah's lower lip trembled. "I know, but he's my pet."

Stephen set his fork on his plate. "A snake is not a pet. It is a wild animal. Wild animals are *not* pets, and they do not belong in this house."

Reine's chest tightened as she watched the child's expression turn sad with disappointment. Snakes were definitely not her favorite animals, but she knew that Jonah loved Chester as much as any human could love a slithering, green, six-inch-long reptile.

"He's not in the house," Jonah said. "Reine gave him a home, so now he can stay on the back porch."

Stephen turned his dark eyes toward her. "You gave that creature a home?"

"A box. An old shoe box that I didn't need anymore." Her explanation held more defiance than she'd intended. "Chester had to have a place to stay."

"Chester is a snake." His quiet words echoed off the walls of the dining room.

Reine felt in awe of his power and authority for a few moments, but then, regaining her senses, she remembered the challenges that poor Jonah and his siblings were facing in their young lives. If a little grass snake helped ease Jonah's grief at such a terrible time, then she could see no harm in his keeping it as a pet. Why was Stephen being so inflexible?

She inhaled a deep breath. "Yes, he is a snake and Jonah's pet. He needed a better place to live than the pocket of Jonah's cargo pants."

Stephen's brows lifted a fraction of an inch higher. "His pocket?" He turned back to his nephew. "You put that snake in your pocket?"

"It's my job to keep my pet safe."

"He is not a pet."

Reine felt her temper rising. She disapproved of Stephen's

persistence of the issue with a five-year-old. With effort, she kept her opinion to herself as Mrs. Saunders entered the dining room with a tray of coffee and dessert.

"I hope you like cherry cobbler."

"With chocolate sauce. Yum!" Peter licked his lips and accepted a bowl.

Unlike his brother, Jonah ignored the final course of the meal and crossed his arms in front of his little chest. "Chester is so my pet, at least until I get a different one. I'd like a pet mouse or a guinea pig. When I get one of those, then I'll let Chester go free."

"Jonah, you cannot have a rodent as a pet."

"A guinea pig's a rodent? Well, then I want a puppy."

"Oh, yes," Peter agreed. "A puppy, Uncle Stephen. May we get a puppy?"

Sarah clapped her hands covered with sticky cherry cobbler and chocolate sauce. "A puppy! A puppy!"

As Mrs. Saunders poured coffee for Stephen and her, Reine imagined the three children playing with a puppy in the yard and thought it was a wonderful idea. When she glanced at Stephen again, he was shaking his head.

"No puppy. No pets. We have enough problems to solve at the moment."

"Oh, please, Uncle Stephen." Jonah kneeled on his chair and leaned toward the head of the table until he wobbled over his bowl of cobbler. "Just a little one."

"No, Jonah."

The child's lower lip trembled again. "Then I'm keeping Chester in his shoe-box house on the back porch."

Reine watched Stephen's eyes darken, and she held her breath. Was he going to argue with Jonah all evening?

"You have a telephone call, Mr. Morley."

Mrs. Saunders stepped back into the dining room. "It's Gwyneth Coulter. She says it's important."

Wiping his mouth with his napkin, he rose to his feet and turned to Reine. "Excuse me. I'm sorry I have to take this call, but I'll try to make it quick."

As his uncle hurried from the dining room, Jonah dug a spoon into his bowl of cherry cobbler. "Will you read to us before you leave, Reine?"

Catching his napkin as his elbow pushed it off the edge of the table, she smiled down at the little boy. "If your uncle says it's okay, I'll read it before I go." She had read his favorite book so many times that she was certain she could recite the whole story from memory. "We'll have to ask him."

"Oh, he'll say yes." A shadow crossed the child's face. "Uncle Stephen likes the puppy story more than he likes Chester." Then his face brightened. "Look at Sarah."

Peter giggled. "She fell asleep in her cherry cobbler."

Reine looked at the little girl with her head propped on her arm on the tray of her high chair. "I think she needed that nap she didn't get today."

"Oh, my, my." Mrs. Saunders shook her head as she entered the dining room. "That poor child is tired right out."

Reine stood up from her chair. "I'll clean her hands and face if you'll tell me where to get a washcloth."

"Stay and finish your coffee. I'll get a washcloth for you. Jonah, Peter, when you're done with your cobbler, you can help me clear the table."

"Let me help."

"You're company." Mrs. Saunders waved a hand at Reine. "The boys like to help me, don't you? It'll be enough if you take care of Sarah."

When the housekeeper returned with a warm, wet washcloth, Reine set to work wiping butter, vegetables, cherry juice, and chocolate sauce off Sarah's face and hands. Although the little girl sighed a few times, she did not open her eyes. When Reine brushed bread crumbs and pieces of green beans off the child's shirt and lifted her into her arms, Sarah snuggled against her shoulder and continued to sleep.

"See, Reine. Sarah likes you so much. Won't you please take care of us?"

Jonah nodded at his brother's words. "I know why Sarah likes you. It's the way you smell."

Mrs. Saunders and Stephen entered the dining room from opposite doors as Reine rounded the table. She kept a secure hold on Sarah as she took her seat again and leaned against the back of the chair.

"The way I smell?"

"Yes." Jonah's blond head bobbed up and down as he swallowed the last spoonful of his cherry cobbler. "You smell really good, likes flowers and sunshine. Sarah likes that, and so do I."

"Put your dishes on the tray, boys. Peter, you're in charge of clearing the glasses. Jonah, collect the silverware." With the boys' help, Mrs. Saunders filled the tray and then headed back toward the kitchen door with them as she shook her head. "Flowers and sunshine. What a character you are, Jonah."

Reine watched Stephen as he took a drink of his coffee. His eyes met hers above the gold-edged rim of the fine china cup.

Her heart did a little somersault. She wanted to look away but fought the urge and held his gaze.

"Sarah looks very comfortable in your arms."

"She's exhausted."

"Would you like me to take her?"

Reine shook her head. "She's fine. Finish your dessert." She reached for her coffee cup. "Everything is all right, I hope."

He appeared puzzled at first. "Oh, the phone call, yes. A minor mishap. Normally, I would be rushing back to my office, but it's almost time for Mrs. Saunders to leave. I'm afraid I am having a difficult time adjusting to my new priorities."

"My grandmother assures me that we get only as many challenges in life as we can manage."

Stephen pulled a hand through his hair. "Your grandmother must be very confident about the plan her life is following. At the moment, I'm having doubts about what the future holds for me. I think maybe I've gotten myself into a dilemma that even strong self-assurance may be unable to get me out of."

Reine shook her head. "Don't lose hope. Things will work out."

"But I know nothing about raising children. I have no idea what I'm doing."

Sarah whimpered in her sleep, and Reine put her coffee cup on its saucer. She patted the little girl's back until the child settled once again.

Stephen gazed at his niece. "I am amazed at how quickly Sarah and the boys have grown attached to you. They think you're wonderful."

"I'm very fond of them too."

He finished his coffee and set his napkin on the table to his left. Silence filled the room as he rubbed his chin and seemed to examine his empty glass.

Reine's heart felt heavy as she studied the fatigue and discouragement in the lines on his face. She wondered what would ever elicit a smile from him. How sad, she thought, that a man could see nothing in his life about which to smile and find joy.

When she lifted her eyes, she already knew he was looking at her, but she was not prepared for the intensity of his scrutiny as she met his gaze. Her heart raced, and the quietness of the room hummed in her ears.

"How important to you is your position at the community library?"

If his intention was to astonish her, he'd definitely achieved his goal. She cleared her throat. "I'm not sure what you mean."

He held her gaze. "Your job. I am curious to know how devoted you are to it."

"I enjoy it. I've always been interested in local history. Being in charge of scheduling events during which authors and other knowledgeable people present history and folklore of the area is very interesting, and researching local family genealogies is a wonderful way to make a living. And then, of course, there are the books. I love to read."

"There cannot be many prospects for advancement in such a position."

"Perhaps not, but there is more to life than promotions and salary raises."

"Do you plan to move away from the area?"

"I'm not sure. I grew up on the Outer Banks. This is home to me. Right now, I have family obligations that keep me here. The volunteers at the library are friendly, energetic people, and the work is appealing. I'm very happy to have a job there."

"Would you ever consider leaving?"

"No, of course not. I need to work."

"I mean, resign from that position to accept a different one."

"At this point, I have no plans to leave my position."

"Not even to work for me here, as the children's nanny?"

She thought he must be teasing. "I have a job."

"How flexible are your hours? Are you able to change the time you start and end your work day?"

Reine felt the muscles in the back of her neck tighten at his exasperating persistence. "My hours must be approved by the village council, but I can set them. Why?"

"I was wondering if you would consider, if not a resignation, then a change in your hours to accommodate an additional position of watching the children at specific times when I have to be at work."

"I'm not a nanny, Stephen."

"I am asking you to be a temporary one." He leaned toward her. "You could split your time between your position at the library and the one here. I know it would make a long day for you, but you could come first thing in the morning, to be here when the children wake up, and stay until Mrs. Saunders arrives."

"I thought you said it was too much to ask of her."

"It is, but she offered to take care of the children during her usual hours, on a temporary basis, of course." His dark eyes pleaded with her. "For instance, you could work from ten to six at the library. That would give you eight hours there, and then you could return here and stay for a few hours to cover the times when I often have to attend meetings in the evening. I'd pay you whatever you ask."

"Money isn't everything."

"You can't work for free. Please say you'll give this plan some thought."

She chewed her lower lip as she rocked Sarah back and forth in the chair. *Two jobs?*

Stephen Morley's determination irritated her, but guilt gnawed in her stomach. She could not forget the child in her arms or the two small boys in the kitchen helping Mrs. Saunders. They needed consistency in their young lives.

She inhaled a long, deep breath that did little to calm her frayed nerves. "Do you always get what you want, Mr. Morley?"

"Not always, but I admit that I do not often resort to begging. Please, Reine. Give me a month. I hope to be able to find a suitable replacement for Miss Eddleton by then."

She sighed again. "It's getting late. I promise to give your offer careful consideration, but I can't make such an important decision tonight. I need some time to think about all of this."

Chapter Seven

Reine did not tell Niles about Stephen Morley's idea that she become the children's nanny. She dreaded the thought of facing Stephen again on Saturday without having an answer to give him, but she did not want to disappoint her brother, who appeared to be looking forward to the casual dinner dance event at Morley Cove Resort.

Her brother had worn navy pants with a white polo shirt and a lightweight jacket, and Reine was proud to accompany him into the bright dining room decorated in a nautical theme with a row of windows that overlooked Morley Cove and Roanoke Sound. Strings of tiny white lights lined the windows both inside and out, and others had been wrapped around the railing along the perimeter of the deck that jutted out onto the water.

Niles led her to a round table where several other local charter fishermen were already seated. While he ordered drinks for them from a waiter, she looked around the busy dining room and noticed Gwyneth Coulter and Jeremy Lawson chatting with other people she knew. Realizing that she recognized many of the guests who were involved in commerce and tourism in the area, she began to feel more at ease.

"Here you go, Reine. Club soda with lemon juice." Niles handed her a tall glass. "Are you sure you don't want something stronger? A glass of wine?"

She shook her head as she took the drink from him. Despite the realization that she knew several people attending the dinner, she could not get rid of the nervous feeling in her stomach.

"Reine."

She recognized the quiet voice before she turned and saw Stephen Morley striding toward her. Swallowing, she tried to think of something intelligent to say.

"Hey, Stephen, it's good to see you." Niles smiled. "This is quite an affair you have going here. I feel as though I should have worn a suit."

Reine studied Stephen in his typical attire of a dark, well-fitting suit, crisp white shirt, and dark tie as he responded to her brother's remark. He always looked so neat and free of creases. With a sigh, she wondered if she should have worn something more formal than her simple twill skirt and floral, short-sleeved blouse.

Stephen shook his head. "I prefer a casual atmosphere. I told my staff to wear informal attire too."

Reine supposed that rule did not apply to the quiet, aloof executive towering over her as he reached out to shake Niles' hand. She could not help wondering how Stephen Morley would look in jeans and a T-shirt.

"Reine?"

She realized that someone had spoken to her, and she had not been paying attention. Feeling her cheeks burn, she smiled. "Pardon me?"

"Stephen was just asking if we'd like to go out onto the deck where some of the wait staff are serving hors d'oeuvres."

She inhaled a deep breath. "Yes, yes, that would be fine."

She had no intention of putting anything in her tumbling stomach right then, but it was easier to agree to the suggestion than to deal with Niles' questions or Stephen's intense, inquiring eyes.

Stephen smiled at her as he reached for her hand. "I have to greet the guests now, but I hope there will be time later for us to have a longer conversation."

Niles nodded. "You promised Jeremy and me that you would discuss that charter fishing proposal we've been working on."

"Ah, yes." Stephen spoke to her brother as he continued to hold her hand. "I assure you that I will sit down later." He turned to her. "I hope to see you too, Reine, after we get the Business Association meeting out of the way."

He released her hand, and she watched him walk away toward the center of the room. Squeezing her hands together, she acknowledged that Stephen Morley had an unforgettable touch. *If only he would smile once in a while.*

"Reine! What are you doing here?"

She turned to see Deborah rushing toward her. Her friend wore a sleeveless cotton dress and sandals and a wide grin on her face.

"Did I just see Stephen holding your hand? Oh, Reine, this is wonderful."

Reine shook her head. "You're impossible."

Deborah glanced around the Pelican Room. "Did you come as Niles' escort for the business and tourism dinner? You won't be able to do that much longer, because soon you'll have your own date to attend such wonderfully exciting events." Her best friend tilted her head toward the group of people talking near them. "It looks as though Niles won't be dateless much longer either. Who's the skinny brunette with the pout?"

Reine followed Deb's gaze. "A person in Nags Head that

you don't know? Wow, your communication system must be breaking down."

Deborah swatted her arm. "Come on. The one standing next to the father of my future children?"

"That's Gwyneth Coulter, Stephen Morley's executive assistant. I think she's from Norfolk."

"It seems as though Niles is a little sweet on her."

"Gwyneth? No, I don't believe it." Gwyneth, the complaining, overwrought Morley Cove staff member who clearly disliked young children was not the kind of person she ever thought her brother would find attractive.

"Just watch the way he's looking at her."

Reine sighed. "He's talking with Jeremy, and she's standing there. That's all I see. Are you going to tell me what you're doing here?"

"Bob Malone had to go to some family function in Kill Devil Hills so he asked me to fill in for him as a representative of the Oceanside Market. Sometimes I really hate being promoted to management. Now I have to do all of the boring public relations stuff that goes along with it."

Deborah grasped her arm and steered her toward the sliding doors leading to the roofed deck. "At least there'll be good food. I'm starving. Let's go get some of those luscious-looking hors d'oeuvres." She grinned. "And maybe later, Jeremy will ask me to dance. That'll make this whole evening worthwhile."

Despite her resolve to ignore the irrefutable presence of the host of the dinner party and Deborah's constant chatter, Reine continued to follow him with her gaze as he rounded the Pelican Room. She watched him stop to talk with the local government leaders and business owners and their escorts. She saw him give instructions to the members of his staff and organize the events of the evening so that the association meeting ran with smooth efficiency from the opening remarks by the mayor, through the buffet dinner and keynote speech, to the closing comments by Stephen himself.

At the end of the dinner, Reine pushed aside her dessert dish of wild berry sorbet as she watched Jeremy Lawson swing Deborah around the dance floor while a lively country tune played. With a sigh, she stirred her black coffee and then smiled when Niles leaned toward her. "This isn't as bad as I thought it would be," she told him.

"See? Getting out and being with people is always much better than sitting around at home with your head in old history books or searching the Internet for lost members of someone's family tree." He squeezed her shoulder. "Do you mind if I ask someone to dance?"

His question startled her. "No, of course not. Who's the lucky girl?"

Niles' blue eyes sparkled. "Stephen's executive assistant, Gwyneth Coulter."

Gwyneth? Reine tried to keep the absolute astonishment from her expression. "Well, go have fun. I'll be fine."

Nodding, he wiped his hands on the linen napkin by his plate and rose from his seat. "You should ask someone. There are plenty of guys here tonight."

"I think I'll just watch the crowd."

Niles and Gwyneth? What an interesting combination. Smiling at the thought, she turned back to her coffee. She did not notice Stephen approaching until he was standing beside her.

"Hey, Reine, hand me my glass of water." Deborah pushed her hair from her flushed face as she and Jeremy approached the table. "That dance took the breath right out of me. Oh, hello, Stephen. You throw a really nice party!"

Reine watched their host's eyes widen in apparent surprise. He held out his hand to shake Deborah's.

"Miss Lyons, I did not see you here. It's a pleasure to have you join us."

Deborah smiled. "I came a little late. Bob Malone called me at the last minute to take his place." She reached for the glass Reine handed her and gulped a large drink of water.

He glanced at Reine and then back to Deborah. "Are the two of you always together? It seems that whenever I see one, I see the other."

Niles chuckled as he and Gwyneth walked up to the table. "It's been that way since they were little girls. At least now, they habitually stay out of trouble." He winked at Reine. "I'm afraid that was not the case when the two were younger. Ask Deb about the time we found them walking on their way to visit her Aunt Alice."

Deborah narrowed her eyes. "We would have made it if you hadn't ruined our plans and stopped us."

"Your aunt lives in Baltimore."

"We were six years old, Niles. We hadn't figured out every detail."

Stephen glanced at Reine. "Walking to Baltimore? I see your transportation situation has not changed much in the last twenty years or so."

Deborah set her empty water glass on the table. "Hey, watch it, Niles Jonson. I have some interesting stories about your mischievous childhood too. Someday I'll enlighten everyone with some of the thrilling adventures you and Jeremy took as reckless teenagers." She grasped Jeremy's arm. "Oh, I love this song. Come on. Let's dance."

Reine watched her friend and her brother return with their partners to the dance floor. She tried to pay no attention to the penetrating dark eyes on her as she stirred her coffee.

"There's a breeze outside tonight. Would you like to join me?"

With trembling fingers, she set her spoon on the saucer. Her thoughts raced as Stephen leaned toward her.

"Oh, you haven't finished your coffee yet."

"It's getting cold."

"I'll have someone bring you another cup."

She shook her head. "No, I mean, I'm done."

She jumped when he reached for her hand. "Will you come with me, then? Just to talk. I need some fresh air."

She felt the same way. The air-conditioned Pelican Room at Morley Cove Resort had suddenly become hot and stuffy.

On unsteady legs, she rose to her feet and allowed him to lead her the short distance to the sliding doors and the nearly deserted deck. A bright moon was shining, and its reflection in the water of Morley Cove gave the evening a quiet, tranquil appearance.

Reine breathed in warm, moist sea air and tried to calm her nerves as she walked with Stephen to the railing along the perimeter of the wooden, unroofed porch with steps leading to the ground. Although he had released her hand, his nearness intensified her senses and made her aware of his every movement.

He leaned against the railing and gazed out at the smooth water of the cove. "I truly detest these public events. I would much prefer to be working in my office."

It was difficult to concentrate on his words, and she swallowed. "Why host them then?"

He sighed. "It's part of owning a business, being part of the community. My father enjoyed entertaining. I'm afraid I inherited my mother's desire to remain private and reclusive."

"Your mother lives away?"

"She resides elsewhere, yes. She has other . . . priorities to deal with at the moment, but she loves the Outer Banks area. I think someday soon she'll return here."

Other priorities? What could be more important than grandchildren who have just lost their parents? Reine had many more questions on her mind, but she did not want to appear too inquisitive, especially about his private life. She peered out at the reflection of the moon on the water.

"How are the children?"

"Well, I hope. That is another reason I should not be here tonight, but this dinner was scheduled before they arrived. Mrs. Saunders kindly agreed to watch them this evening. She even wants to take them to her daughter's on Sunday so they can attend her grandson's birthday party. My housekeeper has been very understanding."

He had not yet mentioned his request that she become the children's temporary nanny. She wondered if that was his intention when he invited her out onto the deserted deck.

"So Jonah's okay after his ordeal of hiding out among the garage sale donations?"

She turned and saw him grimace in the glow of the moonlight and the tiny lights strung around the railing. Had the little boy done something more outrageous than run away and hide in her best friend's car?

"The child is maddening. He has no impulse control. He speaks and acts without thinking."

Reine touched his arm. The expensive fabric of his suit jacket felt soft beneath her fingertips. "He's five. Five-year-olds are impetuous and spontaneous. They're children. They haven't learned to reason and to appreciate consequences. Surely you know that."

Stephen shook his head. "I honestly don't know how my brother coped with parenthood. I think the task is almost too immense for me to handle."

She wondered if he was attempting to make her feel guilty. Deception did not seem to fit with his character, but the man sounded so miserable.

"It's all new to you, Stephen. Give yourself some time to adjust to your new responsibilities."

She could not read the expression in his eyes as he looked at her, but she saw the slump of his broad shoulders and heard the desperation in his voice. He was scared and alone and probably still grieving for his brother. Her heart felt heavy and sad.

"Your brother wasn't raising three children by himself. He and his wife took care of the children together. All at once, you lost your brother and sister-in-law and gained three children who are grieving too."

He nodded as he continued to look at her. "You make some very good points."

She gave his arm a squeeze before taking her hand from the sleeve of his suit jacket. "Don't be too hard on yourself. You need to get to know them first."

"You seem to have a natural way with my nephews and niece. I'm afraid I inherited my father's propensity for intolerance when dealing with children."

"What about your mother?"

"She was always much more patient and compassionate."

"Maybe you inherited her kindness and don't even know it yet."

"Sensible and encouraging. What a charming combination."

In the evening light, she thought she saw his eyes darken. She definitely heard his voice deepen.

"You had better be careful, Reine. You could make yourself indispensable."

What does that mean? She jumped when he touched her hand.

"Let's go back inside. I'll get you a hot cup of coffee."

As Reine stepped back into the Pelican Room with Stephen, she noticed that many of the Business Association members and their guests had left. Only a few individuals still sat at the tables around the dance floor.

Niles beckoned to them as they approached their seats. "We think we have a great plan to help you start to enjoy boating, Stephen. We want to get you out on the water for some non-threatening fun."

Jeremy smiled. "Niles has offered to take us out into the Sound on Sunday for some swimming and a picnic lunch. You can see what kind of ride our guests may take without getting nervous being out on the ocean."

Reine watched Stephen narrow his dark eyes at his Director of Guest Affairs. "I am not nervous about being on the ocean."

Niles glanced at Jeremy. "Oh, we know. We just thought you might start to feel better about fishing if you began to enjoy boat rides in general."

"This is your business proposal? To lure me to a picnic on the deck of a boat?"

Niles grinned. "No baiting. No casting. No fishing. At least not on Sunday. My plan, of course, is to eventually get you out to the Gulf Stream fighting with the biggest blue marlin you ever saw. You're going to love it."

"I certainly doubt that. I have no time for such trips."

Deborah grasped his arm. "Oh, come on, Stephen. It's just a little boat ride. I'm going to make my famous potato salad and homemade spinach and herb bread."

He lifted his brows above dark eyes. "You're coming too, Miss Lyons?"

Deborah's head bobbed up and down. "With Gwyneth and Reine. Three guys. Three girls. A perfect balance."

Stephen pulled out a chair for Reine. "I don't usually take time for leisure excursions." He locked his gaze with Reine. "Even if they are perfectly balanced."

"Well, I think it's about time you did." Deborah grinned. "Certainly you can take off one afternoon to have a little fun, and we promise we won't let you go near a fishing rod."

Chapter Eight

You can't back out now, Reine. It's too late."

Deborah pulled on her arm as Reine chewed her lower lip and stared at her worn canvas bag on the floor of her apartment. She had to decide soon. Her brother was waiting for them in the driveway.

"Come on. It'll be fun. We'll all have a great time."

Reine sighed as her friend shoved a beach towel into her hands. Did she want to spend the afternoon with Stephen Morley on the deck of one of Niles' fishing boats?

The idea of seeing him again definitely had appeal. She could not deny that she was attracted to the handsome, quiet man, but he was not the kind of person she saw as relationship material. On the other hand, he was exactly the person Deborah had in mind for her.

"What did you make?"

Reine pointed to the covered plastic dish on the low table in front of the couch. "Fudge."

"Not chocolate, I hope. Stephen doesn't like chocolate."

"He doesn't like chocolate ice cream. We don't know about fudge. Anyway, it's butter cream."

"What is?"

"The fudge. I made butter cream with pecans."

"Perfect." Her friend tossed a faded sweatshirt at her. "What else?"

She had not made up her mind about watching the Morley children. Although she was impressed that Stephen had not tried to discuss the subject with her at the dinner dance on Saturday night, she still did not know if she wanted to commit to a month of working for the man. She was beginning to care about Stephen Morley, and becoming his employee would only complicate matters.

Deborah handed her a bottle of sunscreen and a canvas baseball cap. "There. I think you're all set. Grab your bag, and let's go."

Reine sighed as she lifted her bag onto her shoulder. Stephen Morley affected her in a way no other man ever had. She could not explain the odd sense of warmth and mystifying mix of feelings she experienced whenever he was near. She could not explain why she had not been able to push thoughts of him from her mind the previous night when she was trying to sleep.

"Reine?"

She realized that Deborah had continued to talk to her while her mind had wandered once again to the quiet, tall man who never smiled. "I'm coming." She closed the door behind them. "Are we meeting everyone at the pier at Oregon Inlet?"

"No, Niles is picking up everyone at the resort, and we're riding out together in his van."

Reine's heart fluttered in her chest as she gazed up at the bright blue sky and thought of seeing Stephen again. "It looks like it's going to be a nice afternoon."

She spent the ride to Oregon Inlet just south of the village of Nags Head in the far backseat with the cooler and picnic basket. From up front, she heard Jeremy, Niles, and Deborah chatting about the clear day and chance of storms during the following week.

Gwyneth sat in the seat behind Niles and stared out the window. Her Capri pants and silk blouse did not seem like proper attire for a boat ride, but Reine admitted that she was no expert on fashion as she looked down at her own faded denim shorts and worn seersucker camp shirt over her one-piece tank swimsuit. She preferred to dress for comfort.

Stephen was also quiet, sitting in the passenger seat next to her brother. He had waved to her as he'd stepped into the van but had said nothing. Conversation from two seats away was nearly impossible, so Reine looked out at the busy Sunday traffic and enjoyed the short ride to the pier where Niles moored his fleet of charter boats.

"Grab the cooler, Reine," Niles called back to her as he pulled the van into the parking area. "I'll get the back door for you."

She secured her hair with an elastic band and grabbed her canvas bag. When the back door opened, she jumped down to the asphalt surface and grasped the handles of the large plastic cooler filled with bottles of juice and soft drinks on ice.

"Let me carry that."

Stephen's quiet voice sent a thrill through her, and she looked up into his dark eyes as his long arms reached around her. She swallowed and shook her head.

"I've got it. Thanks."

He would not release his gaze, and she could not pull away from it. "At least let me help." He took a handle on one end of the cooler.

"Oh, don't worry about being chivalrous with Reine." Deborah rounded the corner of the van. "Her name may mean *queen*, but there's nothing elegant and dainty about her. She's been hefting coolers for Niles and her grandfather since she learned to walk."

Reine felt her cheeks burn with embarrassment as she watched Stephen lift his brows above wide dark eyes and continue to gaze at her. Sometimes Deborah did not know when to be silent.

Without another word she took the other handle and led the way along the dock until they reached the far end, where they boarded Niles' wooden, century-old yawl. The fore and aft masts rose high without sails above the spotless, polished deck.

The yawl was Reine's favorite, the one her grandfather and father had salvaged and restored years ago, long before she and Niles were born. Now the boat belonged to her brother. She smiled as she watched obvious admiration cross Stephen's face as he stepped on board. His father may have been instrumental in spoiling the sport of fishing for his son, but the younger Stephen had apparently not lost his respect for a superior vessel.

With the assistance of his one-man crew, a marine biology student from Wilmington who was working with him for the summer, Niles steered the yawl out of Oregon Inlet and down into the calm waters of Pamlico Sound. Powered by its inboard motor, the boat skimmed along the water in the hot July breeze until the thin strip of Hatteras Island disappeared from view and they were surrounded by the sea on all sides.

They ate on a blanket spread out on the front deck. The conversation was lighthearted and friendly. Niles and Jeremy shared with the group the interest they'd had in boating since they were very young. Growing up on the Outer Banks, they always had plenty of opportunities to spend time on the water.

After they finished lunch, Niles offered to take the guests belowdecks for a tour of the small living compartment there. Reine wandered to the railing and gazed out at the awesome expanse of water separating Hatteras Island from the mainland of North Carolina.

"Do you think anything's biting?"

Reine turned to see Deborah walking toward her with a fiberglass fishing rod in her hands. "What are you doing with that? Niles and Jeremy gave us strict orders not to go anywhere near the fishing gear today. They're trying to convince Stephen to consider establishing a fishing charter fleet for the resort."

"Oh, pooh! Do you really think I'm afraid of your brother and Jeremy?" She cast the line over the port side of the boat. "We're on a *fishing* boat, aren't we?"

Reine climbed up onto the railing and perched there looking over the edge. "I haven't seen a single fish yet today."

"Neither have I, but I'm still trying." Deborah leaned against the railing and adjusted her cap on her head. "I can't figure Stephen out. Can you imagine not liking one of the most popular sports of the area when you own a tourist resort as big as Morley Cove? He's just got to get over his lack of interest in fishing."

Reine recalled what her grandfather had told her about the times he had taken Stephen's father out fishing with his young sons. Perhaps Stephen disliked the sport because of the unhappy memories he had of fishing with the man who should have made sure his sons enjoyed it.

"Uh-oh. Here he comes now."

Reine turned as Deborah began to reel in the line. In khaki pants and short-sleeved tan oxford shirt, Stephen Morley strode toward them.

"What seems to be the problem, Miss Lyons?"

Holding the fishing rod behind her, she pivoted on her heels to face him. "The fish don't seem to be biting today. What are you doing sneaking up on us like that?"

"I never sneak up on anyone." He turned to Reine, who was still sitting on the railing, and locked his eyes with hers. "I came to enjoy the view."

The view? You're not talking about the water, are you?

"Oh." Deborah followed his gaze. "Oh. Sure. Well, if you'll excuse me, I'll just take this pole over to the gear trunk. I'm, um, not catching anything anyway."

Reine heard Deborah rush around the side of the deck. Swallowing, she looked up as a seagull swooped down near her and cawed.

"Aren't you afraid sitting up there?"

His question was quiet and close to her ear. She wondered if he could hear her heart thudding against her chest.

"Of what? Falling in? The water's warm, and I'm wearing my swimsuit." She tucked her bare feet around the bottom railing for better balance. "I was actually thinking about jumping in on purpose."

"Don't you dare."

"Why not?"

"Because you might bump your head."

Reine felt a twinge of embarrassment as she remembered bumping her head at the Creamy Scoop. "I'm not always so graceless."

His dark eyes widened, and he shook his head. "I don't think that at all. I'm simply not dressed for rescuing."

"Well, you don't need to worry, because I don't need rescuing."

She looked out over the huge, smooth surface of the sea and sighed. "I used to think I could swim all the way to the mainland."

"An aspiration?"

"No, more like a childhood whim. I never even tried it."

"Swim to the mainland? I'm surprised."

"Why?"

"Because you impress me as a very determined young woman. I imagine that Reine Jonson can accomplish anything she wants."

"And by *determined*, you mean *obstinate*?"

"Not necessarily. The two words have entirely different connotations."

She watched another seagull swoop toward the deck of the boat. She was unaccustomed to having silence between them, but she did not feel uncomfortable. Perched on the railing of her brother's yawl, she was enjoying the beautiful afternoon and the presence of the man beside her.

He surprised her when she felt his hands slip around her waist and settle there. Warmth from his touch seeped through the thin fabric of her shirt and swimsuit. Thoughts of sharing a cone of plain vanilla ice cream with him raced through her mind.

"I was wondering if I might try a piece of the fudge you made for the picnic. I was much too full earlier to have dessert."

Fudge? No, she was thinking about ice cream. With a deep breath, she turned to look at him. "Of course, but I think I should warn you that it's very sweet."

She watched his eyes darken in the sunlight. She felt his hands move down to her hips.

"As sweet as the cook who made it?"

Was he flirting with her? She smiled. "That sounds very poetic. I thought you were a more practical type."

He held her gaze. "Perhaps. I'm afraid I am out of practice making conversation with a woman I find attractive. Recently I spend most of my time discussing business or speaking with young children."

You find me attractive? Her breath caught in her throat. Was it possible that he liked her as much as she liked him?

"If I promise to stop using terrible poetic phrases, may I try your fudge?"

She held her breath as his hands lifted her from the railing of the yawl. Swallowing, she nodded. "You don't have to promise, but I think that poetic similes are probably wasted on me.

Anyway, few people who know me well would ever describe me as sweet."

His hands still rested on her hips as he urged her toward him. Her head whirled as she watched him lower his own until his lips touched hers. His brushed her mouth with slow caresses that sent tingling sensations to every part of her body. She could not breathe or move. She could only feel.

Too soon, he lifted his head and heaved a deep sigh. "Oh, Reine, you're wrong. You are very sweet."

With trembling hands, she gripped the yawl's railing. *Sweet?* What was he talking about?

He set his hands on her shoulders. "And I am definitely not a poet, but I believe *sweet* describes you perfectly."

She cleared her throat. "I . . . I left the rest of the fudge down in the galley."

Chapter Nine

Another sleepless night did not help Reine make up her mind about watching Stephen's niece and nephews. She spent hours considering the benefits and drawbacks of accepting such a position. In the end, she based her decision on the merits of practicality and hoped that she was not making the biggest mistake of her life.

Locking the file cabinets in her office Monday afternoon, she checked her calendar for Tuesday's schedule before finally making a brief call to tell Stephen's secretary that she was on her way to Morley Cove Resort. This time she walked straight to the second floor of the main lodge without stopping at the front desk. As she passed the playroom, Jonah darted out and skidded to a stop just inches from her.

"Reine, you're here. Please take me home with you."

She squatted in front of the little boy. "What's wrong?"

"I have to check on Chester. He must be lonely in his box on the porch."

"Oh, I'm sure Mrs. Saunders talks to him when she can."

Jonah wrinkled his nose. "I don't think she likes Chester very much."

"Not all people like creepy crawling creatures as much as you do, Jonah. How are you today? Did you tell Robbie you're sorry for hiding from him?"

Jonah's expression was solemn as he nodded. "And he even read the puppy at the farm story. Right now we're drawing pictures. Do you want to come in and help?"

Reine looked past him into the quiet nursery when Robbie smiled and waved to her from his seat at one of the low tables. "I really can't, Jonah. I have to go talk with your uncle right now. Where are Peter and Sarah?"

"Peter's helping Jeremy work on the computer. I wish I could help, but Uncle Stephen says I'm too little to play with all the buttons on the keyboard." Jonah wrinkled his nose again. "He's afraid I'll break something. Sarah's with Gwyneth, but I don't think she's happy. Gwyneth's not too happy either."

Reine hid a smile from the little boy whose observations of the world were remarkably keen for such a young child. As she stepped into the reception area, Sarah's crying filled the room.

With tears streaming down her face, the small girl stood next to Terry's empty desk while Gwyneth talked on the telephone across the room. Reine met the pretty but distressed blue eyes of Stephen Morley's executive assistant.

"Reine!" Sarah flung herself at Reine's legs.

Covering the mouthpiece of the receiver with her palm, Gwyneth pointed a long finger at Sarah. "Can you do something with her? She never stops crying."

"I hurt. See?" The little girl stuck out her elbow so Reine could look at the small spot where the top layer of skin had been scraped. "I falled."

"Poor little Sarah." She lifted the child into her arms. "Where did you get hurt, sweetie?"

Sarah flung her arms around Reine's neck. "Outdoors. It hurts. Owww!"

Gwyneth ended her call and replaced the receiver. "She fell hours ago, but she's still crying about it. I honestly don't know what to do with her."

Sarah burst into tears. "I hurt."

"It's okay, Sarah. We'll find something to make your arm feel better."

With a long, slow breath, she turned to Gwyneth. "Is there a first aid kit nearby?"

Gwyneth nodded as she reached into a drawer of the desk. "I took her down to the resort clinic, but she screamed so much that the nurse couldn't help her."

Reine felt Sarah stiffen in her arms as Gwyneth set a small plastic container on Terry's desk. The little girl peered at the box with suspicion.

Reine removed a tube of antibacterial cream with her free hand. "I think this medicine will help your elbow feel better." She used a quiet, soothing voice as she spoke. "Sit down here on the desk and let me look at it."

"Is there something I can do?"

Reine shook her head at Gwyneth as Sarah stiffened. She squeezed a small amount of antiseptic ointment onto a tissue from the box on Terry's desk. Replacing the cap, she held the tube out to the little girl.

"Here, hold the medicine for me, Sarah."

While the child was distracted by the tube, Reine dabbed the cream on her elbow. "There, that didn't hurt much, did it?"

Sarah's lower lip trembled, but she shook her head. "Pick me up, Reine."

Reine smoothed blonde curls back from Sarah's tear-stained face before lifting her into her arms. "There, sweetie. Do you know where Peter is?"

The little girl nodded. "To get juice."

"They've been thirsty or hungry all day long. Terry left me here in the office with both phones while he went to get snacks for them."

Reine inhaled another long, deep breath and kissed Sarah's forehead. As the little girl snuggled against her, Reine turned to Gwyneth. "I'm here to see Mr. Morley."

"I know." She nodded at Reine and gave her a slight smile. "He told me to have you wait in his office. He'll be back from the finance committee meeting downstairs soon."

Reine patted Sarah's back. "Is it okay if we just sit here at Terry's desk?"

Gwyneth shrugged. "It's not as comfortable as Stephen's office, but you may sit wherever you want. I'm going to forward the calls down to the front desk while I take a break."

Reine heard Gwyneth's heels tapping on the hardwood floor as she left the suite of rooms. Sarah's quiet breathing and the low music of a radio on the other desk were the only sounds reaching her ears as she sat holding the child.

While she waited, she glanced around the reception area. On an adjacent wall hung an oil painting of Morley Cove Resort, with its large expanse of property and numerous structures set along the waterfront of Roanoke Sound. The view was breathtaking and gave her a sense of tranquility.

"I'm sorry to have kept you waiting."

The sound of Stephen's quiet voice pulled her attention from the picture, and she smiled. "I haven't been here long."

"Where is Gwyneth?"

"She said she needed a break. She didn't seem very happy when she left."

"You and your understatements, Reine. Gwyneth is extremely upset with me right now. Earlier today, she even threatened to quit."

Reine smoothed the blond curls of the child in her arms. "Because of Sarah?"

He nodded as he gave her a steady look. "How do you do that?"

"What?"

"Sarah has been fussing all day. Then she spends a minute with you and, miraculously, she falls asleep."

Reine shifted in the chair. "I guess she was just ready for a nap."

He set his briefcase on the desk in front of her. "I'll take her now."

She shook her head. "Let's not disturb her too much. Do you have a place where I can put her down? She'll probably rest better that way."

"Yes, of course." Rounding the desk, he grasped her elbow as she rose to her feet.

As he guided her toward the closed door of his office, she breathed in the fresh, woodsy scent of his aftershave and swallowed again. She forced her legs to walk with steady steps into the large open room.

When she entered, she felt as though she were stepping into an immense, rustic cabin. A large plain wooden desk of polished cherry stood at one end against a wall of rough-hewn logs. At the other end, next to a set of French doors through which she saw the sun flashing on the surface of the calm waters of Morley Cove, was a worn leather sofa.

She patted Sarah's back and then set the child on the smooth cushions. "What a beautiful office. It's like stepping into one's own private sanctuary."

"It can be, when I don't allow the worries of the world to follow me in."

He swept his arm toward the matching leather chairs in front of his desk. "Please sit. Would you like something to drink?"

Shaking her head, she took a seat. She waited as he settled into the other chair and leveled intense eyes on her.

Her heart thudded against her chest, and her head spun. The speech she had prepared, the words she had chosen to deliver her response, fled from her mind. She had wanted to sound intelligent and businesslike, but his nearness unnerved her. All she could think about was the way he had kissed her on the deck of the yawl.

In the end, she struggled to speak in simple sentences. She was determined to keep the meeting, and her mind, on the subject of short-term employment. There would be plenty of time afterward to consider the possibility of a relationship with Stephen Morley.

"I've decided to accept the position of temporary caregiver to the children, Mr. Morley, but only if we can agree on a few conditions."

If he was surprised by her statement, he showed no outward sign. "Go on."

She folded her hands in her lap. "I'll watch Peter, Jonah, and Sarah before and after I go to work at the library, but I may have to take them with me to check on my grandparents sometimes."

"Are you sure your grandparents won't be bothered by three energetic youngsters?"

"Actually, they're looking forward to meeting them."

Stephen shook his head. "I hope they're not too disappointed. The three together can be a bit overwhelming at times."

"They both have had some health problems, so I like to make sure they're okay."

"Of course, then, by all means, take the children to check on your grandparents whenever you think it's necessary. I hope you don't plan to bike or walk there. You're welcome to use my vehicle."

"No, that won't be necessary. I'll just need three appropriate safety seats for the children."

"I'll make arrangements for them."

She squeezed her hands in her lap until her knuckles turned white. It was difficult to talk when his complete attention was focused on her.

"Is there something else?"

She swallowed as his quiet words urged her to continue. For a moment, she regretted her decision to accept his offer. Working for Stephen Morley would probably lead to nothing but trouble, but then she remembered the numerous repairs her car needed. If she was going to pay for them, or the down payment for a new one, without her brother's help, she had to take a chance that she was not making a mistake.

With resolve, she forced air into her lungs. "About my wages."

"Yes?"

"I promise to work for the next four weeks to give you time to find and hire a permanent nanny."

He nodded. "I'm not sure what childcare providers in the area receive, but I'm prepared to pay you Miss Eddleton's salary of one thousand dollars per week plus an additional five hundred a week to help offset the inconvenience this is causing you. I fully appreciate your willingness to help us in this difficult situation."

Reine thought she must have misunderstood the amount. *One thousand five hundred dollars? For one week?*

She shook her head. "Not that much. I couldn't." She stared at him. "Are you serious? That was what you were paying Miss Eddleton?"

"She also received room and board, but I assumed that you would be returning to your own home at night."

Reine's thoughts raced. With such financial incentives, it would not be difficult for Stephen to replace Miss Eddleton, and because of his generous wage offer, Reine would be able to replace her car and save for graduate school.

She inhaled a long, steady breath. "I was wondering if it would be possible for you to pay me in advance for my first week." She watched him lift his brows above dark questioning eyes. "That is, if you wouldn't mind. There's something I need to take care of."

"I will write you a check immediately. Is that everything?"

She raised her head. "I had a question about Saturdays."

"If you can watch the children for part of the day, I would be grateful. Saturdays are the only time I have to get any personal business done. I should be finished with my obligations by early afternoon, so you would be able to leave then."

"I already promised the Youth Group that I would help collect garage sale donations until noon this coming Saturday."

"Ah, yes, you still prefer to use your time instead of taking monetary donations."

She wondered if he was teasing her. She felt a little thrill rush through her at the thought of sharing a casual joke with him as she did with her other friends, but she saw no hint of a smile on his handsome face.

"Please don't change your plans. Just come by the house when you're done."

"Thank you. And I don't work Sundays."

"I would not expect that. Are you prepared to begin tomorrow morning, then?"

Reine chewed her lower lip and debated about whether or not to push Stephen Morley's generosity any farther than she already had. Silence hummed in her ears.

Finally, she mustered the courage to make her final request. "There's just one more thing."

"Yes?"

"It's about Chester."

"The snake?"

"Jonah's pet."

"A snake is not a pet."

"Jonah considers him one. I'll start tomorrow and watch the children six days a week for a month, or until you hire a permanent nanny, *only* if you allow Jonah to keep Chester in your house until he and Peter get a more appropriate pet."

"I have already made it clear to the boys that a pet is out of the question."

"But they want one."

"Children do not always get everything they want."

"But Jonah and Peter *need* a pet. Having an animal to love will do them good."

His eyes darkened. "We will have to see about that."

"So, Jonah may keep Chester?"

She watched a thin, white line form along his jaw. She held her breath and hoped that he would not force her to back down from her final demand.

"Am I to understand that you would give up the benefits of a lucrative second income for a slithering, green reptile?"

Reine shook her head. "Not for a reptile. For a little boy's happiness. No amount of money is worth that."

Several long moments passed. She waited on the edge of the leather chair.

He rubbed his chin. When he pulled his hand away from his face, Reine was relieved to see that the tight skin and white line along his jaw had relaxed. She caught her bottom lip between her teeth and waited as her stomach twisted into tight knots. Had she requested too much?

His voice was quiet and controlled when he finally spoke. "Very well, Reine. We have a deal."

"Jonah keeps Chester?"

"Jonah keeps Chester."

She felt the tension in the back of her neck relax, and she

held out her right hand to him. "Okay, then, Mr. Morley, I'll be at your house first thing tomorrow morning."

The heavy weight of concern she had been carrying disappeared when she cashed her first check from Stephen and walked to Don Jenkins' garage to pay for her car repairs. She was delighted to learn that the vehicle would be finished and ready for her to pick up by the end of the week.

The tension in her stomach relaxed for the first time in days and she began to enjoy her new responsibility to the three Morley children, although she still worried about keeping in check her growing feelings for Stephen. No matter how hard she tried, she could not get him, or his kiss, out of her mind.

After she finished work at the community center on Friday afternoon, she secured the three new child safety seats Stephen had bought into the backseat of her newly repaired car, and then loaded Peter, Jonah, and Sarah into them before driving to her grandparents' house. Julian and Bernadette greeted the children with warm smiles at the front door and ushered them into the kitchen for milk and fresh-baked cookies.

"Hey, what's going on out here?" Niles appeared in the doorway of the kitchen. "I was planning to take a nap, but how can I sleep with all this chattering keeping me up?"

Jonah's blue eyes were wide as he stared at Reine's brother. "You're too big for a nap. Even I'm too big for one. Sarah's the only one who gets tired during the day."

Niles grinned down at the little boy. "And who are you?"

The child pointed to his chest. "I'm Jonah Morley. That's my brother Peter, and there's my sister Sarah. Who are you?"

Niles tousled Jonah's blond hair. "Morley?" He glanced at Reine. "Stephen's niece and nephews?"

"They're having dinner with us tonight." His grandmother smiled. "Jonah, this is Niles, Reine's brother."

Jonah glanced up at Reine. "You have a brother? Wow! This is great!" He turned back to Niles. "Will you teach me how to catch a baseball with a mitt? Uncle Stephen is too busy, and Reine's pitches aren't very good."

Grinning, Niles narrowed his eyes at the child. "What about my nap?"

"You can sleep later, when it gets dark. Won't you show me, please?"

"Come on, Niles." His grandfather rose from his seat. "Let's take these boys out to the backyard. I'll show Peter my garden while you and Jonah practice some pitches and catches with your old ball and mitt. They're in the storage shed."

Jonah took Niles' hand. "How about fishing? Can you teach me to hold the rod?"

"Look! The rain stopped." Jonah pointed out of the large windows of his bedroom.

Reine stepped over Peter and Sarah, who were arranging toy race cars on a plastic track on the floor, and followed the child's gaze out at the grass and shrub-covered yard behind the Morley house. "But everything is still very wet. See the puddles everywhere?"

He tugged on her arm. "You and Peter and I can wear boots, and you can carry Sarah. Let's go play outdoors, Reine. I'm tired of staying in the house."

Reine smoothed the hair on his blond head as he grasped the edge of the thin, white curtain. "Now, you know Sarah won't let me hold her while you and Peter are splashing around on the ground."

"She'll just have to get her shoes muddy then."

"And mess up Mrs. Saunders' nicely mopped floors?"

His blue eyes gleamed as his little sister approached them. "Let Sarah go out without shoes. That way she won't ruin her sneakers *or* the floor. Hey, Peter and I can too. Then we can wash our feet off under the hose before we come back in."

Sarah kicked off her shoes. "I splash too."

Reine lifted the little girl into her arms and smiled at Jonah. "Boots are a better idea. Let's go find some, and then we can splash in some puddles."

Mrs. Saunders directed them to a wooden storage area under the back porch that was full of gardening supplies, empty clay pots, and several pairs of worn rubber boots. Although most of the footwear was too large for any of them, the children did not complain. Giggling, they pulled on old green boots and then found a pair for Reine.

Trees, hedges, and bushes were still wet from the heavy morning rain and ocean mist as the little group wandered along the perimeter of the Morley property. They ventured into the grove of pines and oak trees on one side and looked at wild-flowers and insects. They listened to the sounds of seagulls and other birds.

Sunlight began to filter through the branches of trees lining a path toward a narrow stream that flowed into the cove. Jonah and Peter ran to the water ahead of Sarah and Reine.

"Be careful, Jonah. Don't slip on those rocks. Everything's still wet."

Reine watched as the little boy stumbled and then fell with a splash onto his stomach into the bed of the shallow stream. As Sarah jumped up and down and Peter tried to grab his brother's arm, Reine rushed across the rocks at the edge of the water to pull the child to safety.

Struggling to his feet, Jonah wiped muddy hands on his T-shirt and grinned. "Hey, we could swim right into the cove from here."

Peter shook his head. "Uncle Stephen told us not to go swimming in the cove unless he said we could."

"Are you hurt, Jonah?" Reine ran her hands down his arms and legs.

The child giggled. "No, I'm just wet, Reine. Stop worrying."

She pulled Jonah to her and hugged him. His shirt was dripping with water, and it soaked the front of her sweatshirt.

Sarah clapped her hands. "More, Jonah! Belly splash again!"

"No, Sarah." Reine shook her head and made her way with care back to level ground. "No more belly splashing today."

"Hey, what's that?" Peter pointed toward the cove. "It looks like a dog."

Before Reine could respond, Peter and Jonah scrambled up the side of the stream and headed across the wet sand and grass. She caught Sarah's hand as the little girl began to stumble in her oversize boots.

Lifting the child into her arms, Reine hurried after the boys. With concern, she watched as they slipped and sloshed on the saturated grass and disregarded her warnings to stay away from the stray animal near the water's edge.

"It *is* a dog, Reine. Look! He's friendly."

Still several feet from them, Reine ran as fast as she could in loose rubber boots and a child in her arms. "Don't touch him, Jonah. We don't know that dog."

As she approached the cove, she saw that the animal was a large golden retriever with a red nylon web collar around his neck. He bounded over to meet the boys.

"Oh, he's so cute." Jonah rubbed the dog's ears as Peter patted his wet fur.

Sarah wriggled out of Reine's arms. "A doggy. Pretty doggy."

Reine noticed a metal tag hanging from the dog's collar as she tried to catch Sarah's hand and keep the child from the dog, but she missed. The little girl squealed in delight as she rushed toward the golden retriever.

The dog pushed past Jonah and ran to Sarah. As the little girl wobbled and fell down on her back, the wet animal leaned over her and sniffed her face. Then he licked her cheek, and she giggled.

Reine hurried to rescue her, but Sarah wrapped her arms around the dog. The golden retriever licked the child's face again and then lifted his head.

Before Reine realized what the dog was doing, he shook himself and flung water from his drenched coat all over them. Watching the scene in disbelief, she saw the laughing boys fall onto the ground beside their sister. The dog barked and ran around the group of children rolling on the wet sand.

"What is going on out here?"

Chapter Ten

Silence hung in the air as the quiet question stopped the children in the middle of their romping. The three stumbled to their feet. Even the golden retriever halted near Jonah as the little boy set a hand on the dog's head.

Reine swallowed as she turned to see Stephen Morley striding across the yard toward them. She glanced at the children while she pushed back wet strands of hair that had worked their way loose from the elastic band at her nape.

All three of the children were wet and covered with sand and clumps of grass and mud. One of Sarah's boots had slipped from her foot. Reine's sweatshirt was soaked from Jonah's fall in the stream. *What a mess!*

With a sigh, she raised her gaze and dared to meet the intense, dark eyes directed at her. Stephen's jaw was firm, and, as usual, he was not smiling.

For a moment, she worried about what to say to him, and then she grinned. She could not help it. The situation was so ridiculous, it was funny. To the neat and proper businessman in his suit and polished leather shoes watching them, the group must look absurd. Unable to help herself, she allowed her grin to turn into a full smile.

Jonah caught her eyes, and he smiled also. As he began to laugh, Peter did too, while Sarah clapped her hands and jumped up and down with one foot in a boot and the other covered with a sandy, wet sock.

The dog barked and jumped against Reine. Surprised, she lost her balance and fell to the ground. The air filled with more peals of laughter from the children.

Without a word, Stephen held out his hand and helped her to her feet. She enjoyed the warmth of his touch despite the solemn look he gave her, and her heart quickened. Then all the children started speaking at once.

"We've been exploring, Uncle Stephen."

"Jonah fell in the water, but Reine checked for broken bones."

"I don't have any. Broken bones, I mean."

"Pretty doggy."

"May we keep him, Uncle Stephen?"

Reine reached out to examine the metal tag on the retriever's collar. "This is Teddy, and there's a phone number. I'll bet his owner is looking for him."

Peter patted the dog's back. "Hi, Teddy. Did you run away from home?"

Stephen lifted Sarah into his arms. "He may have been frightened by the storm this morning and gotten loose. His family will be worried."

Jonah hung his head and kicked the ground with the toe of his rubber boot. "I thought we finally had a real pet. Too bad Teddy can't be ours."

Reine slipped her arm around his small shoulders. "Teddy already has people who love him, Jonah. We have to call to let them know he's okay. Come on back to the house." She retrieved Sarah's boot from the ground. "We'll get some towels and try to dry him off a bit before he has to go home."

Jonah's eyes brightened. "Maybe we can find a snack for him."

"And some water." Peter fell into step beside them. "Maybe he's thirsty."

"The dog is soaked. I doubt that he needs water."

Reine could not tell by his tone if Stephen was amused or upset. She glanced at his profile as he walked next to her, but she was unable to read the expression on his face.

On the back porch, Stephen helped the children take off their boots while Reine went to the laundry room for towels. When she returned, Jonah and Sarah were feeding the golden retriever cheese-flavored snack crackers. Peter carried a bowl full of water from the kitchen sink.

With his arms crossed, Stephen watched as he stood a few feet away from the scene. Sandy footprints covered the stone floor of the porch, and boots and socks were scattered everywhere. At that moment, Teddy decided to shake again and sent water spraying in all directions, including Stephen's.

The children squealed and then hugged Teddy, who seemed to thrive on the attention, while Stephen remained silent. His face was grim as he met Reine's eyes.

Handing the pile of towels to Peter, she unfolded one and attempted to pat some of the water from the retriever's saturated golden coat.

Jonah tipped his head and looked up at his uncle. "I guess we made a little mess."

Reine stopped wiping the dog's fur and turned to see Stephen's brows rising above unreadable, dark eyes on his unsmiling face. "A *little* mess?"

"Well, a big one." Jonah smiled. "But we had so much fun.

You should have come with us, Uncle Stephen. I jumped in twenty puddles and fell in only one."

"Not counting the stream, right?" Peter laughed as he wiped Teddy's hind legs.

Sarah giggled as the dog licked her face. "Hold still, Teddy."

Jonah laughed and turned back to his uncle. "I even splashed water right over the top of my boot once. Reine says that puddles are made for splashing. I didn't know that, Uncle Stephen. Did you?"

The little boy's uncle caught Reine's gaze. "No, I was unaware that puddles existed for splashing."

Jonah bobbed his head up and down. "And woods are made for exploring, and rocks for climbing, and pets, like Teddy, for loving."

"Reine said all of that?"

Jonah grinned. "Well, I made up that last part myself, but I'm sure it's true. Pets are here for us to love."

Stephen glanced around the porch. "And so they can make messes like these to clean up, no doubt."

Peter patted the golden retriever's back. "After Teddy goes home, we'll clean up the porch, won't we, Reine? Mrs. Saunders won't have to do it."

His uncle unfolded his arms and dropped them to his sides. Reine noticed the wet spots and sandy marks that Sarah must have made on his suit jacket. There was even a grass stain on the cuff of his otherwise pristine white shirt.

"Mrs. Saunders isn't here."

Reine rose and wiped her hands on a clean, dry towel. "Is something wrong?"

He nodded. "I'm afraid so. Her daughter had to go to the hospital again. The doctors are worried about the baby. I told her to take as much time as she needed until both her daughter and the baby are out of danger."

Jonah threw his arms around Stephen's leg. "I hope Mrs. Saunders' daughter is okay." He tipped his head, and tears spilled from his eyes. "I hope she doesn't die. People die in hospitals. Poor Mrs. Saunders."

Reine's chest tightened as Jonah sought comfort from the unpredictability and sadness that had filled his young life. She met Stephen's eyes as his expression of hopelessness seemed to send a silent plea for assistance across the room to her. She was not sure what bothered her more, Jonah's quest for solace or Stephen's obvious vulnerability and helplessness in such a situation. She wanted to wrap her arms around both of them, but she swallowed as she fought back her own tears.

Forcing a smile, she knelt next to Jonah and took his little hands in hers. "Not everyone dies in the hospital. It's a place that helps people. My grandpa went to the hospital to have an operation, and he's so much better now."

Jonah sniffed. "He got better so he could work in his garden?" He wiped his eyes with the back of his hands and turned to look up at Stephen. "Grandpa Jonson has a garden, and he likes snakes and worms and bumblebees. He gives seeds to the birds."

Reine smiled up at the tall man. "My grandfather believes in coexisting with nature."

She was relieved to see that the look of sorrow and helplessness was gone from Stephen's face, but she wished that he would smile. Would she ever see one on his face?

"Ah, coexistence. That certainly explains your incredible tolerance of non-human creatures." He glanced at the golden retriever. "We'd better call Teddy's family to let them know he's safe."

Jonah pulled away from Reine. "They'll be worried, I guess. Let's go, Uncle Stephen."

*   *   *

After the young couple, who lived just a few miles from Morley Cove Road, arrived to claim the golden retriever, Reine ushered all three of the children into the kitchen. As they drank glasses of milk and snacked on fresh fruit, she shook her head.

"It looks as though we need baths *before* dinner tonight, kids. We're all really grimy."

"I couldn't agree more."

Reine glanced at Stephen, who was standing at the counter cutting seedless grapes into pieces for Sarah. He had taken off his suit jacket and had rolled up his shirt cuffs. "I didn't splash in a single puddle, and *I* need a shower."

He set a small bowl filled with bits of purple grapes in front of his niece. "As soon as you finish your milk, Peter, go run your bath. Do you think you can manage on your own?"

The child looked up from over the rim of his glass. "I'm eight, Uncle Stephen."

The tall man nodded and turned to Reine. "Then I'll help Jonah in my bathroom if you'll take Sarah to the one in the nursery. As soon as Jonah's done, I'll shower so you can leave."

Jonah climbed down from his chair. "Why can't I take my own bath?"

Stephen looked down at the little boy. "Because you have to pass inspection."

"Inspection? What's that?"

Stephen held up a finger in the air. "Is the shampoo washed out of your hair?" He held up a second finger. "Did you wash behind your ears?" He held up a third one. "Did you clean your neck, back and front?"

Jonah wrinkled his nose. "Okay, okay. I get it. Hey, what about dinner? If I have to wash everything, I'm going to be really hungry after my bath."

Peter stood up from his chair. "You're always hungry."

"That's because I'm growing. What's for dinner?"

Stephen sighed. "Mrs. Saunders didn't have time to prepare anything. We'll probably order out for pizza or sandwiches."

Jonah shook his head. "Reine can fix dinner. She's a good cook. She and her grandma made us a really great meal the other night."

"Reine has already stayed longer than she should have."

"But she came late. She had to do her garage sale work first, remember?"

"Jonah Morley."

Reine smiled at the little boy before turning to Stephen. "Jonah's right. I did come late. I'll be happy to stay and prepare dinner for you. It's no problem."

He leveled his eyes on her. "We'll manage."

She watched him look at her damp, muddy sweatshirt and jeans. At least she had kept her socks relatively clean.

"I don't mind staying, but do *you* mind if I use Sarah's bathroom to clean up a little? I have a change of clothes in my car."

"You actually prepared for splashing in puddles today by bringing extra clothes?"

Although she found no hint of a smile on his handsome face, the sound of his voice was light and lacked its usual somber tone. His question caused her stomach to do a little somersault.

"No, I did not *plan* to splash in puddles this afternoon, but I *did* worry that I would get dusty and dirty collecting donations for the youth group garage sale." She smiled. "That's the reason I have clean clothes in my car, and after I shower, I'll prepare dinner for you and these hungry children."

After a simple meal of shrimp salad, seasoned rice, banana bread, and fresh vegetables with ranch dip, Reine offered to take the sleepy children upstairs and help them get ready for bed. When she returned to the dining room a few minutes later, the table was cleared and the room was empty.

Stepping into the kitchen, she saw Stephen standing at a

counter with his back to her. For a moment, she watched as he scooped coffee grounds into the coffee machine. She felt contented and lighthearted seeing him performing such an ordinary task; but, at the same time, she could not ignore the uneasiness she felt that she was not a part of the life she was observing. In fact, she didn't know if she ever would be.

"So, are they down for the night?"

She forced a smile and crossed the ceramic-tiled floor to open the dishwasher. "Sound asleep. All three of them."

He handed her a pile of plates. "Fatigue certainly did not seem to affect their appetites."

She arranged the dinner plates in the bottom rack and then took the bowls he passed to her. "My grandmother always says that a meal with no leftovers is the sign of a healthy family."

He patted his stomach. "Then the Morleys must be a very healthy group indeed. I ate much more than I actually needed and will have to run at least two extra miles tomorrow before work. Dinner was delicious, Reine. Thank you."

She nodded and took a handful of silverware from him. "I'm not sure what Mrs. Saunders had planned, so I just threw some things together."

"We all enjoyed it."

He met her eyes as he held out two drinking glasses, one in each hand. "You're an excellent cook and an even better nanny, although I am not sure I necessarily approve of some of your approaches to child care."

Reine held the glasses Stephen had handed her. "Which methods exactly?"

"I know you believe that the children should have a pet, but sneaking one onto the property to tug at my emotions is a little underhanded, don't you think?"

She reached out and touched his left arm. "I know you don't honestly believe that I contrived to lead Teddy here, so why don't you tell me what's really bothering you?"

His shoulders dropped. "Peter and Jonah can't stop talking about that animal. They think that retriever is their best friend. Jonah spent his whole bath time making plans to visit Teddy."

"A pet is not a bad thing."

The lines across his forehead deepened. "I have no idea what I'm doing, Reine. Children are a complete mystery to me. They are a commitment I'm not sure I can handle, and now they're determined to add another complication to this mess we're trying to call a family. Of all things, they want a pet."

She gave his arm a little squeeze. "I guess I don't understand what's so wrong about the children having a dog to love. Why do you disapprove of pets?"

Reine watched a shadow cross his face. She waited in silence during the long moments until he spoke again.

When he did, he held her gaze and squared his shoulders. "There is nothing wrong with pets. I just think that having three children to raise is enough responsibility for me to handle right now. I know you think having a pet will help them get used to all the changes in their lives, but I'm not so sure."

Reine smiled. "I believe that if you're patient, you'll see that the added burden of taking care of a pet, with the boys' help, will balance out in the end. You'll see the children grow happy and well adjusted because of it."

"But in the meantime, training a puppy will take time and commitment. I have three children. I think it would be poor judgment on my part to take on another important and time-consuming obligation when I'm barely managing the ones I have."

She gave his arm another gentle squeeze. "I think you're being too hard on yourself."

"And I think you're too optimistic." He held his right hand out to her. "Shall we call a truce?"

"A truce?"

"Let's agree that we have a difference of opinion regarding the particular issue of the Morley children getting a pet."

She looked down at his outstretched hand and then held out her own. "I can't. I have butter on it from the dishes."

"That's okay. I have crumbs on mine from the banana bread." He grasped her hand and gave it a firm shake.

A jolt of sensation rushed to every nerve in her palm. She felt her breath catch in her throat.

He continued to hold her hand in his, even though it appeared to her that the handshake was finished. He had stopped moving his own up and down.

Was he going to kiss her again? She struggled with a mixture of expectation and apprehension. She was his employee at the moment. She could not allow her developing feelings for him to interfere with the job she had agreed to do. She had to make sure her relationship with Stephen Morley remained appropriate.

Finally, he released his hold on her. "I guess that makes us partners."

She swallowed as the strong smell of brewed coffee filled her head and made her dizzy. "Partners?"

"You know, we go together, like bread and butter." His face held no hint of a smile, but she was sure his voice had one. He released her hand and picked up two more drinking glasses from the nearby counter.

She moistened her lips. "Oh, I get it. Bread and butter." She inhaled a long, steady breath as she tried to forget the effect of his touch on her.

Had he experienced the same intense feelings? With shaking hands, she reached for the glasses he held out to her.

"I must say, though, that I find your puddle philosophy intriguing."

"I thought we agreed on a truce." Her fingertips brushed against his, and her nerves danced once again.

"We did. I was just making an observation."

She squeezed dishwashing gel into the dispenser and then closed the door of the machine. When she stood up to her full height, she realized how tall Stephen was and how daunting he could seem. Was he still upset with her?

She swallowed. "An observation about puddles?"

He reached up into a cupboard for two ceramic mugs. Her gaze fell on the tanned forearms sprinkled with fine, dark hair. He set the cups on the counter in front of the coffeemaker.

"I find your choice of activities for children very interesting."

"You have concerns?"

He filled both mugs with hot coffee. "About puddles? No, just curiosity."

"Oh, come on. I've never met a child who didn't like to splash in puddles after a storm." She shook her head as he offered to add cream and sugar to her cup. "When you were younger, you weren't drawn to puddles after a rain shower?"

He handed her a mug of black coffee and then leaned against the cupboard while holding his own cup. "No, I don't recall ever having a fascination with puddles. Did I miss some important stage in my childhood development?"

She gazed at him over the rim of her cup. Her eyes caught a sparkle in his eyes that she had never noticed. "Probably."

He lifted his brows. "Are you serious?"

She nodded as she smiled at him and then sipped the strong, hot liquid. "At least, as far as puddles go. In fact, the next time it rains, I'm going to have you put on rubber boots and join the children in the yard. You can learn to play in the rain and enjoy puddles just like you should have when you were little."

"Please explain how my getting muddy and soaking wet will benefit me now."

"Adults need to learn to have fun, especially when they are raising young children."

She watched a shadow cross his face. In his dark eyes, she saw the same disillusionment and hopelessness that she had observed earlier that day when he had tried to comfort Jonah. Her heart felt heavy. Being rich and successful did not make Stephen Morley a happy man.

"My father did not share your beliefs regarding child rearing. He never splashed in rain puddles, nor did he allow my brother and me to engage in such a carefree activity."

With her free hand, she reached out and touched his arm. "That doesn't mean you can't start now."

She felt his muscles flex under her fingertips as they touched the taut skin of his forearm. She wished in desperation that she could think of something encouraging and consoling to say to him.

"Well, anyway," he said after a deep sigh, "the children obviously enjoy your choice of activities. To our advantage, they've fallen asleep at a reasonable hour."

She removed her hand from his arm as he offered to refill her coffee mug. The sudden loss of physical connection created a strong sense of disappointment. With a trembling hand, she held out her cup to him.

"Jonah and Peter were tired of being cooped up indoors. They can't stay in the house all day just because the weather doesn't cooperate. I believe that their keeping active will help the grieving process they're going through right now more than anything else they do."

Stephen set the glass carafe on the warming plate of the coffee machine and picked up his mug from the counter before turning back toward her. "How do you know so much about all of this?"

"All of what?"

"Grief. Sadness. Have you had many losses in your life, Reine?"

"Some. My father died when I was three, and my mother, when I was fifteen, but my brother and I have been fortunate. We had wonderful grandparents to raise us and care for us."

"Three years old? That's awfully young. Do you remember your father?"

She stared down into the dark coffee in her mug. When she finally raised her eyes, he was watching her. The warmth in his expectant gaze astonished her.

"No, not as well as I'd like. I mean, we have lots of photographs, and my mother used to tell my brother and me stories about him. My grandparents still talk about him now and then, but that's not really the same as having my own memories."

"Do you have any clear recollections of him?"

His words were soft and urging. She realized that she liked the sound of his voice. Although it could be cool and indifferent, it also had a soothing quality that could calm her and put her at ease. She wanted to share her memories with him.

"I remember a big man who had a deep, joyful laugh and strong arms that lifted me in the air and wrapped around me in loving hugs. He had a beard that tickled when he kissed me on my cheek."

She smiled. "Horatio Niles Jonson was his name. Like my mother, he grew up right here on the Outer Banks. Ancestors on both sides settled in this area years ago. He and Mom met in kindergarten and married as soon as they finished high school."

"Niles is older, right?"

"Yes, by five years. Dad was a commercial fisherman. He died in a storm just off Cape Hatteras in late October. I remember Mom crying for days. We moved in with Grandpa and Grandma soon after the funeral."

He lifted his brows above sparkling dark eyes. "Despite losing your father at an early age, I'll bet you were a fascinating child, Miss Jonson."

She grinned. "By fascinating, Mr. Morley, I hope you don't mean difficult. I would like to think I had some lovable qualities, as well."

"Oh, I have no doubt you had lovable qualities. In fact, you still do."

Her heart thudded against her chest. She watched him tip his head to one side.

"I thought we agreed that you would call me Stephen?"

"That was before I became your employee."

He set a hand on her shoulder. "You're more than an employee, Reine. I have entrusted the precious lives of my niece and nephews to your care."

Thoughts raced through her mind in confusion. The air in the large kitchen seemed too thin.

She forced herself to breathe, but the action almost hurt. Moistening her lips, she avoided his eyes. "I should go."

Stephen watched from the front door of his beach house on Morley Cove as Reine drove down the driveway in her old red car, and then sighed as he headed toward his study with his cup of lukewarm coffee. Reine Jonson was an exceptional individual. He was going to have a difficult time finding a replacement for her. That idea bothered him more than ever now that he had spent the evening with her. *Why?*

He had hired her only until he could find someone qualified for the position of nanny. She had accepted the temporary job of taking care of the children only because he had promised to find someone as soon as possible to replace her.

Why did the idea of finding another individual to take her place create such heaviness in his heart? Why did the thought of not seeing her with the children, her big brown eyes filling with wonder or surprise and her quick smile flashing with delight, cause him to feel sad and dissatisfied?

As he sat down behind his desk and tried to concentrate on work, he shook his head. Jonah was right. Reine smelled like flowers and sunshine, and Stephen was having a hard time getting that thought out of his mind.

Chapter Eleven

Face it. Stephen Morley likes you."

Deborah fell in step beside Reine as she headed for the Nags Head Community Center the following Sunday morning. A humid breeze rustled the leaves of the tree branches overhead, and the hot sun heated Reine's face and arms. "And you reach that conclusion based on what?"

As Reine hurried along the sidewalk next to her friend, the flowing skirt of her floral sundress brushed her knees, and her feet felt comfortable and warm in white leather sandals. What a gorgeous summer day!

"On the way he looked at you when we were on the boat last Sunday. On the way his eyes sparkled whenever he saw you at the business dinner. On the way he always wants to be alone with you."

"How do you know he wants to be alone with me? Anyway, he never smiles. What kind of a man has nothing to smile about?"

Deborah grinned. "A tortured one, but you'll make him

smile someday. Just wait and see. Do you think he'll come to the brunch this morning?"

"I think so. I mentioned it to him, and Jonah and Peter are looking forward to it. I hope something doesn't come up unexpectedly. The children will be so disappointed if they can't come."

"Over here, Reine! Come sit with us!"

Jonah's shouting invitation echoed through the community center dining room as he waved both arms in the air. Reine could not help but smile as she watched Stephen struggle to calm the little boy. She and Deborah approached the Morley family sitting at a table near one corner.

In a two-piece charcoal gray suit and crisp, white shirt, he rose as they set their trays next to empty seats around the rectangular table. After Reine introduced the children to Deborah, they sat down and began to eat.

Deborah smiled at Jonah, who was bouncing in his chair. "Did you get enough to eat?"

The youngster grinned. "Not quite yet, but everything's yummy!"

Stephen glanced at his nephew as the little boy took a huge bite of cinnamon roll. "How is the fund-raising coming along, Deborah?"

"Very well, thanks." Deborah cut a sausage link with her fork. "The sale donations we collected yesterday were incredible. We have quite a large variety of items to sell. The Youth Group should make an adequate amount of money to redecorate the whole children's library and buy a supply of new books."

"I'm glad to hear that."

Reine took a drink from her water glass and looked at the quiet, dark man sitting across the table from her. She watched Stephen wipe Sarah's small hands with a napkin before he turned to meet her eye, and her heart fluttered.

"I think I may have something to donate."

"Really?" Deborah said. "That's great!"

"I have come to realize that you were right. Everyone has something that he or she is no longer using. In the past, it has just been easier for me to make a monetary donation rather than to bother with actual articles."

Reine smiled at Stephen. "I hope you're not thinking of donating Chester."

His intense eyes sparkled as he shook his head. "I'm afraid the Youth Group would have to *pay* someone to take that wild snake."

"Hey, Chester's my buddy." Jonah swallowed a bite of ripe strawberry as red juice dribbled down his chin. "I can't sell him."

Reine patted the child's arm. "Don't worry. We were just being silly."

Deborah nodded. "We usually don't have much call for pet snakes at the community garage sales, but one year we sold a whole litter of baby kittens."

"Kittens?" All at once, Sarah appeared interested in the conversation.

Next to his uncle, Peter nodded. "I like kittens too. Let's get a kitten for a pet, Uncle Stephen."

Stephen narrowed his eyes. "No kittens."

Jonah licked strawberry juice from around his mouth. "We're getting a puppy. Puppies are much more fun than kittens."

From across the table, Stephen leveled his eyes on Reine. "This is all your fault."

She knew he was teasing her because his tone was almost playful. She wondered once again how he would look if he smiled. The attention he was giving her made her feel as though they were the only two people in the room.

She cleared her throat. "You were saying that you found a donation for the sale?"

A silent moment passed as he continued to hold her gaze. She wondered if he was experiencing the same sensation, that they were all alone in the hall and not surrounded by three children, her best friend, and several members of the community.

"Yes." He finally spoke as he pulled his dark eyes from her. "I may have some unused furniture to contribute to your cause."

Deborah finished her glass of juice. "When should we pick it up?"

"There's an old storage barn on my property where I put used articles from the old lodge before I had it torn down. I thought perhaps there may be some wooden items we could salvage for the library fund-raiser."

Reine handed Jonah another napkin as strawberry juice dripped down his chin and onto his white dress shirt. "From your old house? They're probably antiques."

He shrugged. "Is that a problem?"

"You should ask an expert to appraise the items before you start donating them. People who come to the community sale are looking for good, used furniture. They may not appreciate the value of a two- or three-hundred-year-old table or chair."

Stephen lifted his eyebrows. "It was my understanding that you ladies were more interested in the charitable aspects of a contribution than in its monetary value."

Deborah's head bobbed up and down again. "Well, you're right, but we don't want anyone to get cheated, either the people who buy the things or the ones who donate them."

"I understand your concern, but I really have no interest in the value of the old things in the barn. There may be an item or two that someone could use. If you would be willing to search through the clutter, you may take whatever you find for your sale."

"Oh, we couldn't possibly choose without your consent."

"You have my consent."

"I think Deborah means that we wouldn't feel right just selecting items without your final approval on the furniture we choose. Why don't we look together?"

"I detest dusty, dirty places. That is why I have avoided venturing out there before now. If you want any of those items, you will have to search for them without me. I'll concede to inspecting your final choices, if that will relieve your anxiety."

Deborah took a drink of juice. "That sounds better. Reine and I will plan a time to snoop through your unused stuff. What fun! In fact, I may have a few minutes tomorrow to look at what's there. I'm taking a half day off for a dentist appointment in the morning. If I have time, I'll stop by before lunch."

"Mrs. Saunders has the key."

Deborah rose from her chair. "Well, I've really got to run. We're having my father's family reunion picnic down at my uncle's beach house in Avon this afternoon." She patted her stomach. "More food. Just what I need."

Reine and the members of the Morley family said goodbye, and then Deborah hurried toward the nearest exit. Reine wiped her hands with a napkin before gathering the used plates and glasses.

"Wow! A picnic!" Jonah swallowed the last bite of his sticky sweet roll. "I wish we were going on a picnic at the beach."

Stephen looked at his nephew. "A picnic after what you've eaten? Don't you think you've had more than enough for one day?"

Jonah's expression was serious. "Maybe enough until lunchtime."

Reine's laughter burst from her before she could stop herself. Tears spilled from her eyes and rolled down her cheeks as she reached out to give the little boy a hug.

"What's so funny?" He squirmed in her arms. "I didn't make a joke."

"I too fail to see the humor of a child who never seems to fill up."

Releasing Jonah, Reine wiped her face and then looked at Stephen, who had rounded the table and was standing near her. His dark eyes held a solemn expression as he gazed down at her.

She studied the angular lines of his handsome face, his firm jawline and his unsmiling mouth, before looking back into his eyes. Her heart fluttered before resuming its normal rhythm. All she could think about was the feel of his lips on hers.

Finally, he turned to his niece. "I need some exercise. What do you think, Sarah? Should we take a walk to the beach?"

Peter rushed to his uncle's side. "Let's go!"

Jonah bounded out of his chair. "I want to run. Let's run all the way to the beach just like Uncle Stephen runs every morning."

"I said walk." Stephen set his hand on his niece's blond head. "Are you ready?"

The little girl's blue eyes looked up at him. "I find puddles."

Stephen turned to Reine. "Do you see what you've started?"

She ignored his teasing query and smiled at Sarah. "I'm afraid all the puddles from the rainstorm yesterday have dried up, but if you take off your shoes, I'm sure your uncle will let you splash in the waves that roll up on the beach."

Sarah slid from her chair. "You come too, Reine."

Stephen turned to her. "Despite the undermining of my authority with your continuous quest to make life *fun* for these children, we would, of course, like to have you join us, but I don't want to keep you from your obligations here."

For a moment, she hesitated. Her emotions were tumbling in all directions, and she was not sure she wanted to spend more time with Stephen Morley, the tall, quiet man who possessed the ability to make her heart race and her head spin.

"Please, Reine. Come for a walk with us."

She looked down at Jonah's pleading blue eyes. He was smiling up at her as he squeezed her hand.

"Where's the beach?" Peter asked from Stephen's side.

"Let's go on a picnic." Jonah jumped up and down. "We can pack sandwiches and potato chips and lemonade and cupcakes. Chocolate ones with orange frosting."

Stephen stared down at his younger nephew. "Chocolate and orange? That sounds horrible. How can you keep talking about food?"

Jonah grinned. "I'm a growing boy."

"Yes, and soon you'll be growing right out of your clothes."

Stephen met her eyes, and Reine wondered if she should have left when she'd had the chance. Her legs felt unsteady as she tried to read the expression on his face, but, except for an almost imperceptible darkening of his eyes, there appeared to be nothing there that she could decipher. Stephen Morley was a mystery to her. Would she ever understand him?

Jonah tugged on her arm. "Let's go back home and pack just a snack, then."

After a long time, Stephen pulled his eyes from hers and looked down at Jonah. "No snack. Just a nice walk on the beach."

The little boy's head drooped. "All right. Just a walk. Where are we going?"

Stephen turned to her again. "Down by the pier? We should probably drive, though."

She nodded. "Instead of trying to cross the highway with the children."

"Do you have your car?"

"No, I walked over."

"You'll ride with us?"

She smiled. "Yes, thank you. I'm all done here. Another group of volunteers is helping with the cleanup."

After the short ride to the beach next to the Nags Head fishing pier, Stephen pulled his large sport utility vehicle into the parking area and helped the children out of the backseat. Soon the little group was strolling along the white sand on a section of the beach that had few sunbathers.

Reine held Sarah's hand and walked beside Stephen while Jonah and Peter ran ahead of them. They walked on the damp, hard-packed sand just at the point where the waves stopped and rolled back to the surf.

Reine breathed in the refreshing ocean air. The hot, bright afternoon sun shone down on her bare arms and face.

"Stay away from the water, Jonah!" Stephen called to the little boy. "You're getting too close."

She shaded her eyes against the glare as she watched Jonah explore the beach. The little boy inched his way toward the powerful Atlantic waves pushing toward them.

"Be careful, Jonah."

"I am. I'm just looking at the water."

Reine gazed across the shimmering expanse of ocean. She allowed the ebb and flow of the water to mesmerize her for a few moments. She always felt very tiny and inconsequential next to the powerful expanse of water.

"Wow!" Jonah said. "The ocean is really big!"

"Look at that boat out there, Uncle Stephen." Peter pointed. "Are they fishing?" He tipped his blond head to look at his uncle. "Is this a good place to fish?"

Jonah bounded back toward them. "Uncle Niles said he'll take us fishing soon."

"Stay away from the edge, Jonah," Stephen said. "Those waves are very strong and dangerous."

Peter nodded. "Uncle Niles said he'd teach us how to cast a line."

"And reel in big fish!" Jonah added. "Do you know how to cast, Uncle Stephen? Uncle Niles said it's really easy once you know how."

Stephen lifted his brows and glanced at Reine. "*Uncle Niles?*"

Jonah looked out over the water as his feet edged closer to the ocean. "Reine's brother. He's a good fisherman, and he knows everything about fishing. His grandpa taught him. He knows when to use worms and lures and soft bait. He says he's going to take us to catch the biggest fish we've ever seen. Don't you want to come with us, Uncle Stephen?"

Stephen reached out to grasp Jonah's shoulder. "I want you to stay away from the edge of the surf. I'm afraid you're going to lose your footing, and a wave will knock you down and pull you under."

"Okay, okay. I'm being careful."

As Stephen picked up Sarah, Reine pointed to the gray and brown bird with a white breast scuttling along the beach. "Look at the killdeer running in the sand."

Sarah bounced on Stephen's shoulders. "A little one and a great big bird too."

Her uncle adjusted his hold on her as she pointed her little finger toward the sky. "Yes, a big one. That's an osprey."

Peter followed his sister's finger. "Look at how far his wings stretch!"

Stephen nodded. "Most ospreys have a wingspan of five or six feet."

Peter said, "I think he's watching us."

Stephen shook his head. "He's probably looking for fish to eat."

Out of the corner of her eye, Reine detected movement. Before she realized what was happening, Jonah followed the killdeer along the sand to a point where a strong wave was headed.

"Uh-oh." The little boy's voice held a tone of nervousness and fear as he stumbled.

Reine's breath caught in her throat as she watched Jonah try to catch his balance. In an instant, she darted forward and reached out to him.

Her grip slipped, but she caught the lapels of his unbuttoned suit coat with her hands. She held on to him as she felt her own feet slipping out from under her and the sand beneath her feet beginning to erode with the force of the wave.

Pulling the child toward her, she attempted to lift him back up to the safety of dry sand as her left foot twisted and her sandal seemed to move in the opposite direction. When her foot turned, a sharp pain shot through her ankle, and her knee buckled.

The incoming wave crashed against her calves, but she held on to Jonah against the strength of the water until the tide rushed back out to sea. She sucked in a large breath of air and tried to steady her racing heart as her ankle throbbed with sharp stabs of pain.

To her relief, she realized that someone was reaching out and taking Jonah from her grasp, but the movement caused her unsteady left leg to slide in the wet sand. Another piercing pain shot through her ankle and up to her thigh.

When she tried to walk, her sandal twisted against her skin and caused more discomfort. Groaning, she fell to the ground.

"Wait. Don't move."

Stephen's quiet voice was soothing in her ear as he leaned down and used gentle arms to help her rise. The throbbing ache took her breath away, and she bit back another cry of pain.

He held her elbow as she attempted to walk. The damp hem of her sundress clung to her lower legs. She swallowed when a wave of nausea sent her stomach into twists and turns. The pain was too great. She could not take another step.

Chapter Twelve

With one hand, Stephen helped Reine hobble up and away from the incoming waves. He eased her down onto dry sand.

She swallowed again and looked around for Jonah. "How is he? Is Jonah okay?"

"He's fine." Stephen was still holding her elbow with one hand and Sarah's hand with his other.

"I was chasing that killdeer." The little boy grinned as he rushed toward her.

Nausea rolled in her stomach even as relief washed over her. "Are you sure you didn't get hurt?"

"I'm sure, Reine. You caught me just in time, but I can't find that bird."

She reached out and cupped his chin with her palm. "You scared me, Jonah."

"I'm sorry. I'm all right, really."

"Everything except his ears."

Reine's eyes darted to Stephen. "His ears?"

"I am going to get the boy's hearing checked." He narrowed his dark eyes at his young nephew. "He does not seem to hear directions very well at all."

Stephen released her elbow. "We'd better be getting back."

She swallowed another wave of nausea and then held her breath as she tried to stand again. Pain brought instant tears to her eyes when she applied even the slightest pressure to her ankle.

"What's wrong?"

She avoided Stephen questioning eyes. "It's my ankle. I think I twisted it."

When she looked down at her injured foot, shock almost overwhelmed her. Her ankle had swollen to twice its normal size. Her head began to spin. She closed her eyes and hoped her unsteady right leg would support her.

"Reine."

Large hands encircled her waist, and then she was no longer standing. Her head rested against the smooth fabric of Stephen's suit coat, and her knees and back felt the heat and strength of his muscular arms holding her.

She felt the rumble of his chest when he spoke. "Peter, take Sarah's hand. Stay right with us, Jonah."

Fighting waves of pain, Reine forced open her eyes. "What are you doing?"

"We're heading back to the car."

"Put me down."

"You're hurt."

She closed her eyes again as pain caused by the movement of Stephen's long strides across the sand stabbed through her ankle and up her leg. A cry slipped from her lips.

"I don't mean to hurt you. I'm being as careful as I can."

She nodded as more tears spilled from her eyes. Humiliation mixed with misery made her wish she could disappear.

"Is Reine all right, Uncle Stephen?"

"She injured her ankle when she reached to catch you."

"She got hurt because she was helping me?"

"That's right, Jonah."

She tried to smile at the little boy who grasped her arm as they moved through the white sand along the beach. She winced at his hold on her. Every nerve in her body was sensitive to touch and movement.

"I'm sorry, Reine. I'm sorry you hurt your ankle," Jonah said.

"Are we going to take Reine home?" Peter asked as they neared the parking area.

"We're taking her to the clinic."

"The clinic?" Reine lifted her head as she felt her cheeks burn. The situation was becoming increasingly embarrassing. "Just take me home, please."

Peter opened the front passenger-side door of his uncle's large sport utility vehicle, and Stephen set her on the seat. His warm breath fanned over her face as he spoke. "You need medical attention."

She held her own breath as he removed his arms from behind her knees and from around her waist. A quiet cry escaped again as he used gentle hands to swing her legs and adjust her feet on the floorboard of the car. Tears rolled down her hot cheeks.

"Peter, help Sarah get into her car seat."

Jonah tugged on Stephen's sleeve. "I want to sit with Reine."

She watched Stephen shake his head. "Get in your seat in the back." He pulled a folded white monogrammed handkerchief from an inside pocket of his dark suit coat and patted one of her cheeks with the square of soft fabric.

After wiping her other cheek, he pressed the handkerchief into her palm. "Just sit back and try to relax. The clinic will have something for your pain."

"The clinic is like the hospital, isn't it, Uncle Stephen? Please don't take Reine there."

Jonah's plea from the backseat took Reine's mind from her ankle for a few moments, but it did not make her forget how close Stephen was standing to her. With one long arm, he grasped the seat belt and pulled it around her until the hook fastened into place. He reached for her hand and locked his eyes with hers.

"It won't be long."

She swallowed as he released his hold and shut the passenger-side door. He checked the children in the backseat and then slid behind the steering wheel. Turning on the ignition, he pulled onto the street.

"Let's go home, Uncle Stephen. We can take care of Reine till she gets better."

"She needs a doctor, Jonah."

"Can't we find her one who'll come to our house, Uncle Stephen?"

"No one can come, Jonah. We have to go to the clinic. It's not far."

"Reine can't go there."

"She has to go, Jonah."

"Please don't make her."

Reine opened her eyes as the little boy's pleas became louder and more insistent. She swallowed another wave of nausea as she attempted to turn around so she could see Jonah, who was sitting in his safety seat behind Stephen.

"Don't go to the clinic, Reine. It's just like a hospital, and people die in hospitals. I know because my mom and my dad died in a hospital. Please don't let Uncle Stephen take you there."

"Jonah, calm down. Reine is not going to die." Stephen's voice was firm but not totally without empathy. "She hurt her ankle. The doctor will examine it and take an X-ray to see if she broke any bones."

Reine forced a smile and reached back to squeeze his knee. "Your Uncle Stephen's right, Jonah. I'm going to be fine."

After examining X-rays of her foot, ankle, and leg, the doctor at the clinic concluded that she had no fractures. When she stepped in the sand to rescue Jonah from the powerful incoming wave, she apparently twisted her ankle, resulting in a severe sprain. Although her injury would not require a cast, it would, the doctor explained, be painful and require specific treatment.

"Will I be able to go to work tomorrow?" Reine leaned forward in the wheelchair in which she had ridden to and from the X-ray area. "If I had some crutches—"

"You'll need to use crutches until you are able to apply normal pressure on your ankle again. That may take a week or more."

"A week? What about my jobs?"

"Stop worrying about work, Reine." Stephen set his hand on her shoulder. "Your health comes first."

He turned to the doctor. "How long do you recommend she stay off her ankle?"

"She needs at least forty-eight hours of rest before she may return to work."

The doctor looked at Reine. "You're going to be in a great deal of pain." He made some notations on the top sheet of a prescription pad and then signed it.

"I want you to stay off your feet until tomorrow afternoon. Elevate your leg and apply ice. Call the clinic if you experience any unusual discomfort or weakness." He tore the sheet from the pad and handed it to her. "Take one of these tablets every six hours."

Reine stared at the paper. *Until tomorrow afternoon?*

"You can have this order for a pain reliever filled at the pharmacy down the street. Don't try to be brave and bear it. Follow the instructions on the bottle."

"She will." Stephen held her gaze. "I'll make sure she does."

"Can Reine go home now?" Jonah had not released her hand since she had returned to the emergency examination area.

The physician smiled. "Yes, son, your mom's all set. She'll need your help for a while."

Jonah grinned. "Reine's not my mother, but I love her just as much. I'll take good care of her."

Reine had a difficult time keeping her eyes open on the short ride home. Despite Jonah's continuous chatter about Chester and Teddy and fishing, she was exhausted from the ordeal and drowsy from the anti-inflammatory drug injection the doctor had given her.

"Shall I take you to your grandparents' house?"

The sound of Stephen's quiet voice roused her from a groggy state somewhere between consciousness and sleep. She cleared her throat. "What?"

"Would you like to go to your grandparents'?"

She gave her head a slow, hesitant shake. "No, no. I should call them though."

"I'm not sure you should stay alone, Reine."

"Grandma and Grandpa would only fuss over me. They have enough to do taking care of themselves. If you don't mind, I'd just like to go to my apartment."

She was afraid he was going to protest, but finally he nodded. "Very well. If you insist."

She closed her eyes and leaned her head against the headrest. The sharp pain in her ankle had subsided to a dull throb.

"Why can't Reine come home with us?"

From the backseat, Jonah's voice startled her, and she opened her eyes. Had she fallen asleep again?

"I think she should stay with us till she gets better. I think the puppy on the farm story will help her ankle."

"Then I suggest you loan her your storybook so she can read it in peace at her own home. Reine would get absolutely no rest with a little chatterbox like you around all the time. She needs a quiet place to relax."

"I can be quiet."

"No, you can't," Peter said. "You're always talking. You *are* a chatterbox."

"Why does everybody call me that? You. Uncle Stephen. Uncle Niles. My name is Jonah."

"Yes, we know." Stephen pulled the vehicle into the sand and gravel drive of Reine's apartment house.

"You remember who Uncle Niles is, right?"

"The man who knows all about lures and bait and catching big fish."

Jonah's blond head bobbed up and down. "He's going to take us fishing someday soon too. He promised."

"I think you'll have to learn to keep quiet first." Stephen unfastened his seatbelt and leaned back to look at his young nephew. "Fishermen don't talk or allow children to talk while they are fishing. Excessive chatter scares the fish."

"Really? Talking really scares them?"

"That's what your grandfather always told me. Now, try to stay out of trouble while I help Reine."

Stephen stepped from the vehicle and retrieved a pair of crutches from the rear hatch. While Reine waited, she slipped the strap of her small purse over her head so it wouldn't slide from her shoulder when she tried to walk.

Stephen opened the passenger-side door and helped her lift her feet from the floorboard to the ground. Handing her first one crutch and then the other, he guided her elbow with his hand as she used slow, awkward movements to steady herself on the unpaved driveway.

Jonah bounced up and down next to her as she began to make her way with care toward the wooden steps leading to her second-floor apartment. He scuffed tiny pebbles into her sandals that increased her discomfort as she tried to walk.

She struggled to maintain her balance, but her attempts proved futile as she began to fall backward. *Oh, no. Not again.*

Her panic subsided when she felt Stephen's hands around her waist. Then, with one arm under her knees and one around her back, she fell against his muscular chest without even a stumble.

"You should not be staying here where you have to climb a flight of stairs to get to your apartment."

"Put me down. I can sit on the steps and scoot up backward."

Stephen appeared to ignore her solution. "Peter, take Sarah's hand and help her."

Jonah tugged on his uncle's arm. "What should I do?"

Reine heard Stephen inhale a long, deep breath. "Take Reine's crutches and carry them upstairs."

"May I try them?"

"No, just hold on to them, and stop bouncing around."

"He didn't mean it." Reine whispered the words as Stephen began ascending the open staircase.

"The child is a menace."

Reine swallowed as she became aware of every movement he made. He seemed to carry her with the ease with which he carried Sarah. He showed no signs of breathlessness or tiredness when they finally reached her door.

"Do you have your key?"

"Right here, in my purse." She felt his muscles underneath the fabric of his suit jacket as she unzipped the leather shoulder bag and pulled out a key ring. The action caused her skin to tingle. With a sigh, she said, "I can walk now."

Ignoring her words again, he used deft movements to take the keys from her hand and slide the correct one into the lock. As the door swung open, Jonah rushed past them into the small living room and dining area.

"I want to stay with Reine, Uncle Stephen. I promise to take good care of her, and I'll be very quiet too."

Stephen stepped through the doorway and strode toward the worn upholstered couch that she unfolded at night and used as a bed. He set her against one end and adjusted her legs on the cushions. After piling throw pillows behind her back, he lifted the strap of her purse over her head and slipped her keys inside the unzipped pocket.

Despite her resolve to avoid his eyes, she looked at him. She could not move or think. She still sensed his arms around her as if his touch had the power to ignite every nerve into sparks of feeling she had never before experienced.

"May I stay with her, Uncle Stephen?"

He blinked then, and she heard his sharp intake of breath. "I'll get you some water so you can take your pain medication."

Jonah reached for her hand as Peter and Sarah moved toward the couch. She forced a smile.

"I'm going to be okay. I just have to rest and stay off my ankle for a while."

Jonah bounced up and down. "How long is a while?"

"Too long, if we don't stop talking and let Reine rest." Stephen stepped around the little boy and handed her the prescription bottle.

She poured a small, white tablet into her palm and reached for the glass of water he held out to her. She swallowed the pill and then allowed him to set the glass on the lamp stand at the end of the couch.

"I think I should call someone to stay with you." He sent a

look toward Jonah. "Someone who is over three feet tall and who does not talk incessantly."

Reine shook her head. "I'll be fine, Stephen." She shifted her position on the couch and forced another smile.

"Rest. Relax. Read a good book." He glanced around her apartment. "This place is extremely small."

"It's big enough for me. At least if I fall, I won't have far to crawl back to the couch."

His eyes snapped back to her. "You have to be particularly careful, Reine."

She sighed. "I was just kidding. You're so serious, Stephen."

"Your health is a serious matter. I hesitate to leave you here alone."

She watched as he pulled a small cell phone from the waistband of his pants. He held it out to her.

"Keep this with you and call me if you need anything at all."

"I have a telephone, Stephen."

"Yes, a wall unit all the way out in the kitchen."

"As you have already pointed out, my apartment is quite small."

He narrowed his eyes at her. "Keep my phone in your pocket."

"I can't take it, Stephen."

He leaned down until his face was just inches from hers and pressed the small device into her hand. "Let's not argue in front of the children." His breath sent heat across her cheek as he whispered the words to her.

The children said goodbye as Reine tried to stay awake. Stephen's final words remained in her mind as she floated in and out of consciousness. "Take good care of yourself, sweet Reine, and I will call you later."

The unfamiliar sound of electronic bells ringing woke Reine from a deep sleep. When she tried to rise into a sitting position by swinging her legs over the edge of the couch, a searing pain shot through her left ankle.

She fought back tears as she reached into the pocket of her sundress and then fumbled to open the flip-style telephone that was making such a noise. She pressed the button with the green light and then lifted the device to her ear as her ankle continued to throb.

"Reine? Are you okay?"

The alarm in Stephen's voice pulled her from her drowsy state. She swallowed and glanced at the empty glass on the table at the end of the couch and the ominous set of crutches leaning against a nearby chair.

"Reine, are you there?"

"Yes, yes." She cleared her throat. "I'm here, Stephen."

She heard his sigh of relief over the telephone. Shifting against the pillows, she tried to move into a more comfortable position. Nothing she did seemed to help alleviate the agonizing pain pulsing through her ankle.

"I told you to keep the phone where you could reach it."

"I did. It was in my pocket."

"It took you such a long time to answer."

"The phone was tangled in the fabric of my dress."

"I thought something was wrong."

She swallowed again and wished she had a cold drink. "I'm fine, Stephen."

"Did you call your grandparents?"

"No, but I will."

"Have you had dinner?"

"What time is it?"

"After eight. You haven't eaten?"

"I guess I've been sleeping. That medicine must be strong."

"I'll get you something."

"No, don't. It's too late to take the children out again."

"I'm not sure you should be alone."

She sat up and stuffed another pillow behind her back. "I'm all right, really. I promise I'll call my grandparents, and I'll eat some soup. Stop worrying."

She breathed through a spasm of pain stabbing at her ankle during the long silence. She hoped Stephen would press her with no more questions. Concentrating was just too difficult.

"I can't seem to stop thinking about you, Reine."

Her heart fluttered and then raced as she realized the implication of his words. Did he truly care about her? It was, of course, quite possible that he was concerned for her welfare simply because she worked for him. But he *had* kissed her. That had to mean something, right?

"Reine? Are you still there?"

She pulled her attention back to the telephone. "Yes."

"Are you sure you don't want me to get you dinner?"

"I'm sure, Stephen. Really."

"I'll stop by tomorrow."

"You don't have to do that."

"Yes, I do. Call me if you need anything, Reine. I'll be right here."

Chapter Thirteen

By Monday morning, Reine was amazed that her injury had improved so much. With the aid of crutches, she could move around her apartment with little difficulty. The discomfort she felt was limited to an occasional pang of pain and a stiffness that was probably the result of a lack of exercise.

She managed to shower and dress in sweatpants and a loose sweatshirt without a problem before folding her bed back into the couch. She replaced the cushions and put her small apartment in order for the day.

Both her grandmother and Deborah had called to check on her. Even Stephen had stopped by during his morning jog to drop off coffee and a bagel. Although he stayed only long enough to make sure she had everything she needed, Reine was touched by his thoughtfulness and concern.

"He brought you breakfast?" Deborah said when she arrived at Reine's apartment just before lunchtime. "Oh, this is getting really good. He definitely likes you."

Reine tossed a pillow at her friend as Deborah took a seat

on the opposite end of the couch. "He feels guilty because he thinks Jonah caused my accident."

Deborah set a small cardboard box on the low table in front of the couch and shook her head. "No, you're wrong. Have you kissed yet?"

Reine wrinkled her nose. She had never told her friend about the kiss Stephen and she had shared on her brother's boat. "I work for him, remember?"

Her friend's eyes glistened with mischief. "Only temporarily. Your status as his employee will change as soon as he finds someone else to be a nanny to those children. Then he'll kiss you. Just wait and see."

Reine eased her ankle from the floor up onto a pillow on the table. "He still hasn't smiled."

"I told you that smiles are overrated."

"He's so serious. His power, money, and success don't seem to give him any fulfillment at all."

"Well, maybe a little glimpse of his past will help him develop some sense of accomplishment." Deborah leaned forward and reached for the small box she had brought with her. She handed Reine a worn leather-bound book. "I went over to his place to check out the furniture he wants to donate. Look what I found in one of the storage rooms in that old barn."

Reine leafed through the brittle yellowed pages. "It's a kind of record book." She looked at her friend. "A ship's log, I think."

Deb nodded. "In the front there's an inscription. Some of the ink is faded, but I could make out a few of the words. The captain's name was Stephen Morley, and he kept this record during a voyage he made from England to the United States in 1853."

Reine thumbed through more of the pages. "The captain must be one of Stephen's ancestors. This is so exciting."

"As soon as you're better, you can go over to the barn and

search through that storage room. I'm done with that dusty, spider-infested place."

"Did you find any furniture that the Youth Group can sell at the garage sale?"

"Lots, but I don't want to make a decision about any of the pieces until you get an expert to assess them." Deborah reached into the box on the table. "There were many more logbooks from Captain Morley's trips. I'm sure you'll find them interesting reading." She rose from the couch. "Well, my morning off is almost over. I suppose I have to get to work. Do you need anything before I head out?"

Reine shook her head. "I'm getting around fairly well now. I think I'll spend the rest of the day browsing through Captain Morley's logs."

Deborah had been gone less than an hour when Reine heard another knock on her door. Engrossed in the seafaring adventures described in the ship's logs her friend had found, she took a few moments to pull her mind back to the present.

"I'm coming." She struggled to her feet and adjusted one crutch underneath her right arm. "It's unlocked. Come in." She wobbled toward the door as it opened.

"Hi, Reine. Are you better?"

Jonah's exuberant greeting sent a wave of warmth through her. She could see his sparkling blue eyes above the enormous bouquet of flowers in his arms.

Her heart jumped when she lifted her gaze to the handsome man behind the little boy. Stephen had changed from his jogging pants and T-shirt of the morning to a charcoal gray suit, white dress shirt, and silk tie that accentuated his somber image of business and success. His dark eyes met hers, and she held her breath.

Jonah jumped up and down. "We came to visit."

"How nice!" Reine reached to swing the door shut behind them and then struggled to regain her balance.

She watched Stephen's jaw tighten as he grasped her left elbow. "You should not be walking so much, and you need to use both crutches when you're up."

His touch startled her. The pressure of his fingers on her arm sent awareness of his closeness through her whole body.

"We brought you flowers."

Jonah lifted the bouquet up to her as Stephen dropped his hand. She smiled as she breathed in the heady fragrance of wildflowers mixed with Stephen's subtle scent of outdoors and aftershave.

"I picked them out, and Mrs. Saunders helped Peter and me cut them."

"They're beautiful, Jonah."

The little boy grinned up at his uncle. "See, I told you she'd like them. They're better than the ones at the flower shops."

Stephen cleared his throat. "Apparently, giving the customary arrangement of roses or carnations is unacceptable to the boy. He declined the entire available inventory on the Outer Banks and opted for the flowers from the garden at home."

"The shops didn't have the right kinds of colors. These flowers do. See? Yellow, orange, purple, white, pink, and red. Just like a rainbow."

Jonah tipped his head to look at Stephen. "They had to be like a rainbow because Reine is pretty like a rainbow."

Shaking his head, Stephen set a hand on his nephew's shoulder and met Reine's eyes. "Although I question the child's choice of floral arrangement, I cannot disagree with his powers of observation."

Jonah grinned. "That means he thinks you're pretty as a rainbow too."

Is that what you think? Reine wished she understood Stephen's thoughts. She cleared her throat. "Let me find a vase for that beautiful bouquet."

She hobbled to the kitchen and opened a cupboard door. As she steadied herself against the crutch, she looked up at the clear vase on a shelf above her head.

From behind her, Stephen reached out and lifted the glass container down from the cabinet. His sleeve brushed her shoulder as he set the vase in the nearby sink and began to fill it with water from the faucet.

She watched as Jonah handed his uncle the flowers, and Stephen arranged the blooms. Squeezing Jonah's shoulder, she smiled. "Thank you so much."

"Uncle Stephen says he's going to work from home. He has his computer and his fax machine and his telephone."

Stephen strode into the living room and set the flowers on the table in front of the couch. "We have to go, Jonah. Reine needs to rest her ankle." He met her eyes. "You are resting, aren't you?"

"Actually, I've been doing some fascinating reading."

She watched him glance at the ship's logs scattered across the couch cushions. His brows furrowed in obvious disapproval.

"It appears to me that you're working."

With her free hand, she picked up a logbook to show him as she shook her head. "It's fun work. I've been reading the first-hand accounts of a captain's sea voyages back and forth from Europe to North America during the mid-1800s. Deborah found them in your barn."

"She did? All of these?"

Reine grinned. "The captain's name was Stephen Morley."

"Stephen has always been a popular Morley name."

"I think this Captain Morley was probably a relative of yours. It seems he did some trading along the Outer Banks and may have settled here at one point."

His dark eyes met hers. "Really?"

As she nodded, a wave of pain stabbed her ankle. She closed her eyes and swallowed.

"Reine."

She felt Stephen's arms slip around her waist and, for a moment, she allowed herself to enjoy his comforting support. With effort, she forced her eyes open. "I'm okay. I just need to sit."

Still holding her with one arm, he slid the ship's logs to one end of the couch. "What you need to do is rest, not research local historical events."

He helped her down onto the couch and propped her ankle on a pillow. "You took the day off from work, right?"

Although his words were firm, his expression was kind and full of concern. Her breath caught in her throat as he reached out to brush back a strand of hair that had fallen across her cheek.

"Promise me you will rest now."

She nodded. "I will."

Jonah threw his small arms around her neck. "Chester really misses you. You have to get better soon."

She smiled. "Give Chester a big hug from me."

Stephen shook his head as he set a hand on her shoulder. "Reptiles do not miss people, and I'm certain they do not appreciate hugs. You are responsible for encouraging the boy's misperceptions."

Reine wrinkled her nose at him and then grinned at Jonah. "Make sure you blow Chester a kiss from me too."

Stephen's sigh of exasperation was exaggerated as he rubbed the back of her neck. "Do you need anything before we leave?"

She enjoyed his gentle caresses and did not want him to stop. "No, thank you."

"You still have my cell phone?"

With a trembling hand, she pulled the telephone from the pocket of her sweatpants and held it up to show him. "I'll be fine."

He seemed to hesitate before he removed his hand from her neck. "Stay on the couch. Jonah and I will see ourselves out."

The following morning, the screen on Reine's laptop computer displayed an alphabetical list of births in the County of New York in 1893. With reluctance, she turned from the small desk in the dining area of her apartment as a knock on the door interrupted her concentration.

"It's unlocked. Come in." She reached for a copy of a document that slid from her printer accompanied by a soft buzzing sound.

"I'm not sure I like the idea of your leaving the door open to intruders."

Glancing up from the paper in her hand, she watched Stephen Morley step through the doorway holding a molded cardboard tray of cups and a small paper bag.

Again she thought he was too big to fit in her small apartment. He towered over the furniture and filled up the room whenever he entered it. Dressed in nylon shorts and a cotton T-shirt, he nudged the door closed with the toe of his running shoe and juggled to keep the tray level in his hands.

She smiled up at him. "You don't look much like an intruder to me."

His expression was stern as he strode toward her and set the tray on the tiny dining room table. "My point is that I *could* be. Honestly, Reine, your casual attitude about your health and safety is infuriating sometimes."

Grinning, she handed him the paper she had just printed. "Look. A copy of your grandfather's birth certificate."

"You're supposed to be resting." He glanced at the paper. "How is your ankle?"

"Good. Great, actually." She rose from the desk chair as she directed his attention to the document. "Your grandfather was born in New York City in 1893. I've found quite a lot of information on the Morley family."

He set the paper on top of the printer. "Why aren't you using your crutches?"

She sighed as she sat back down at the desk. "I can walk just fine without those silly things. They're a nuisance, and I'm ready to return to work too. Both jobs."

He lifted dark brows above penetrating eyes. "Are you sure?"

Kneeling in front of her, he slid her sneaker from her left foot. He ran gentle fingers around her ankle and up and down her calf. "The swelling has gone down, but there's still some bruising. What about the pain?"

She swallowed as heat from his touch made her mind swim with a mixture of confused feelings. She thought again about the kiss they had shared. He could kiss her again. She realized that she wanted him to kiss her again.

She shook her head to clear her thoughts. She worked for him. Another kiss would only complicate matters. When he replaced her sneaker and retied the laces, she dared to breathe again.

"Are you still experiencing any discomfort?"

She moistened her lips with the tip of her tongue. "The pain is nearly gone, except when I put my full weight on it. I'm going back to work tomorrow morning."

Standing, he reached for one of the insulated cups and handed it to her. "I brought coffee and an apple muffin for you."

Reine smiled as she accepted the large cup of black coffee. "You're pampering me. I could learn to enjoy this special treatment."

His dark eyes held hers for a moment. "I could learn to enjoy pampering you, Reine."

He pulled his gaze from her and removed the lid of the second cup of coffee. "Are you sure you shouldn't take another day to recover?"

She shook her head as she took a crumbly muffin from the bag he held open for her. "I think I'm well enough to return to work today, but I don't think I could walk all the way to your house, and my car is back at the garage again."

Holding the bag and his coffee in one hand, he pulled a key ring from the pocket of his shorts. "I drove over this morning. Use my vehicle until yours is fixed."

"Oh, no, I couldn't."

"Why not?"

She tipped her head and studied him. "You drove? Why?" She felt her eyes widen. "You knew about my car? How?"

He set the key next to the monitor. "Niles mentioned that you had to take it to the garage for more repairs."

"Niles talks too much."

Stephen swallowed a bite of his apple muffin. "He's concerned about your unreliable transportation. You should stop being so obstinate."

"I don't need another big brother, Stephen."

Above the rim of his coffee cup, he met her gaze. "I suppose you're right. I apologize. Niles and I were again discussing the possibility of my investing in a charter fleet for the resort. I'm not sure why he happened to mention your car."

She stared down at the black coffee in her cup. "I know he doesn't mean to meddle."

He reached out and rubbed her cheek with his knuckles. "Niles cares about you, Reine. I envy the relationship you have with your brother."

Her face tingled from his gentle touch as she listened to the rich timbre of his voice. He leaned toward her, and she thought he was going to kiss her. She wanted him to do just that, and she held her breath.

When he finally pulled away his hand, disappointment washed over her in recurring waves. She watched him drop his arm to his side.

"Niles has planned a fishing excursion for us today after I return from the office."

Fishing? Reine held her breath. "Who do you mean *us*?"

"Jonah, Peter, Niles, myself. I think Sarah is still a bit too young to go."

Reine tried not to show her astonishment. "It'll be good for all of you to get out and have some fun together."

A shadow crossed Stephen's face, and compassion tugged at Reine's heart. His expression was full of disillusionment, boyish and cheerless, the way his father's harsh words and attitude about fishing probably left him all those years ago.

Although the shadow left, his eyes were still edged with sadness. "It probably does not surprise you that your brother can be very persuasive. With Jonah's assistance, Niles pestered me until I agreed. He promised me the best day I ever imagined."

Reine grinned up at him. "And I hope that's what you have. You deserve some enjoyment in your life." She pushed her chair up to the desk. "Just like my father and grandfather, Niles has fishing in his blood. He learned from my grandfather, who was one of the best fishermen around here, until his heart attack. Catching sea bass is Niles' special expertise."

"Well, I'm holding my opinion until after today's adventure. Angling has never been an interest of mine." Stephen shifted so he could look at Reine's laptop. "My past experiences have been less than satisfying, but I promised Niles that I would keep an open mind about it. Are you going to work here all day?"

Reine clicked the mouse and scrolled down the list of births on the screen. "I think I have enough information to start a preliminary report of your father's side of the family. I'm having a little trouble with your mother's side."

"My family? I thought you were too busy for such an assignment right now."

She smiled up at him. "Hurting my ankle left me with a little extra time."

"If you are so determined to keep busy, we should take you fishing with us. At least then I could see that you were resting your ankle."

She grinned as she tapped out some words on the keyboard. "Oh, no. I know better than to get in the way of a male-bonding fishing day. Hey, why don't you leave Sarah here with me?"

He lifted his brows. "Now, how restful would that be? Chasing a two-year-old all afternoon? Actually, I'm trying out a new sitter. She's the daughter of one of the members of the community choir."

He took a bite of muffin. "Her mother, Nancy Patterson, called me last night because she had heard that I was looking for someone to watch the children."

"I know Nancy. She volunteers at the library sometimes."

"Well, her eldest daughter, Lynn, graduated from high school this spring, and is taking a year off to decide what she wants to do before college. Right now she is looking for a full-time job. Anyway, she has three younger siblings and says she likes children."

Reine clicked to another screen. "So Lynn is going to take care of Sarah?"

"She's willing to stay with her at our house this afternoon."

He sipped his coffee. "I don't want to impose on you, Reine, but if you don't mind, I would like to leave your name and number with her, in case she has any problems."

Reine stopped scrolling and looked up at him. "No, I don't mind, but I'm sure Sarah will be fine." She patted his arm. "Just tell Lynn about how much she likes to rock when she's tired and how she enjoys listening to songs and nursery rhymes."

She turned her attention back to the monitor. "I haven't

been able to locate your mother's birth certificate. Do you remember where she was born?"

"In northern France." His voice was low and near her ear. "Brittany, perhaps?"

"Do you know the town?" Reine typed the information into a search box and waited as a map of the northwestern region of France popped up on the screen. "Let's see. Nantes? Brest? Rennes? Do any of these places sound familiar?"

"I think it had a religious name." His breath was warm on her cheek.

Reine shifted in her seat as she inhaled the faint masculine scent of soap and fresh air. "Saint-Malo? Saint-Pol-de-Léon?"

"No, I don't think so."

"Saint-Lô?"

"There. Saint-Nazaire. That's it." He pointed at the screen.

Reine's breathing stopped as his arm brushed against her hair. She could not move, could not think.

He cleared his throat. "Saint-Nazaire. That's where my mother was born."

Reine blinked. Her heart thudded in her chest as she tried to concentrate. "Saint-Nazaire, a leading French port city at the mouth of the Loire River," she read with a shaking voice. "You're sure?"

Stephen nodded. "That's it. Yes."

She heard his sharp intake of breath as he rose to his full height. Frustration and regret shot through her when he took a step away from the desk.

"I should go."

"Yes, your run." She paused to give her heart a chance to slow its beat. "Thanks for breakfast and for the use of your car."

"My pleasure."

She turned in her chair as she heard him open the door onto the second-floor porch outside her apartment. "Stephen? Your mother's maiden name. I'll need it to research her vital statistics."

His eyes were dark and unreadable as he stood, tall and broad-shouldered, in the doorway. "Desmond. Antoinette Madeleine Desmond."

He closed the door as she was about to ask him for the correct spelling. She had not even typed the woman's first name before the sound of his footsteps disappeared.

"Please, Reine. I want to wait up for him. Please."

Reine tucked Jonah's sheet and blanket under the little boy's chin. "I know you haven't seen your uncle much this week, but it's really late. Look, Peter is already asleep."

She brushed a strand of blond hair from Jonah's forehead. "Maybe you can talk with him before he goes running tomorrow morning."

"I tried that this morning, but he left too early. I have to tell him that Teddy is a daddy and has the cutest puppies. Did you know Teddy had a family when he came to visit us that Saturday after the storm? I miss Uncle Stephen. I miss everybody. I miss Dad, and I miss Mom."

Tears glistened on his cheeks as he slid his arms around her neck. "I love you, Reine. I'm glad you're still here."

Reine sighed as she looked down at the sad expression on the child's face. Stephen had been too busy for everyone since she had recovered from her injury earlier that week, it seemed.

Something was wrong. What had happened to cause Stephen to make such changes in his routine? Why did he seem so preoccupied and quiet? He was spending very little time with the children, and Jonah, especially, was beginning to notice the way he seemed to be withdrawing from them.

As she turned off the lamp next to Jonah's bed, she renewed her determination to speak with Stephen before she left the beach house that evening. She curled up in an old brocade-covered chair in the living room to read the summer of 1858 logbook of Captain Morley until Stephen returned home.

Almost an hour later, Reine woke from a dream in which she was stowing aboard the ship leaving England. Captain Morley had just discovered her presence on his vessel. She forced herself back from a time long ago and looked up into dark, familiar eyes.

Stephen looked for a moment at Reine sleeping in his living room chair. Strands of long, dark hair had fallen over her slender shoulders and across her pale face. Thick lashes curled against her cheeks, and her lips curved into a half-smile. She was always on the verge of smiling. Reine never seemed to have a hard time finding something to laugh about. He loved the sound of her laugh. It made him warm inside and comforted him even on days that were most distressing.

He reached down and fingered a strand of her hair. When she stirred, he pulled away his hand and inhaled a deep breath. "I'm sorry to have kept you so late."

"That's okay." She hid a yawn with her palm. "Is everything all right?"

He dragged a hand through his hair and set his briefcase on the floor next to the chair across from hers. "Yes, things are fine. I've had a lot going on this week at the resort and there have been some personal issues I have had to take care of, but my schedule should start to slow down now."

She closed the captain's logbook. "Jonah wanted to wait up for you. He misses you, Stephen. So do Peter and Sarah."

He nodded as he took a seat and leaned back into the comfortable cushions. "I promise to give them more attention now. I've been in the middle of our triannual review. The accounting department and I were meeting with an independent auditor all week to go over our financial records and make sure everything is in order."

"And is it?"

"In order? Yes, but the whole process is always a less than pleasant experience. I also took some time with Niles to come to an agreement about a regular charter fishing program for the resort. With the assistance of our mutual attorneys, we have worked out a partnership in which Niles provides the charters to any Morley Cove guest who wants to fish. Later, Niles has agreed to help Jeremy and me build up our own fleet right here in the cove."

He watched a smile brighten her tired eyes. She needed sleep. Reine had been working too hard because of his busy schedule.

"That's wonderful news, Stephen." She tapped the book in her lap. "It looks like history *does* repeat itself."

"What do you mean?"

She smiled and moved to the edge of her chair. "I've been waiting to tell you for the past few days now, but you've been so preoccupied. On the journey Captain Stephen Morley made to Norfolk in 1858, he wrote about a first mate who decided to stay in the Virginia area when the captain's ship left to return to Europe."

Stephen felt his anticipation as he watched excitement grow in the expression on Reine's face, her pretty, irresistible face. "Yes?"

"Guess what the first mate's name was?" She grinned. "Oh, I can't wait to tell you. It was Jonson. His name was William Jonson. According to Captain Morley's log, Jonson planned to buy his own boat and become a commercial fisherman. He later settled in the Outer Banks area."

"Is William Jonson a distant relative of yours?"

Reine's smile broadened. "I haven't had a chance to research it yet, but I'm thinking that we're most likely related in some way." She picked up the logbook from her lap. "Isn't that interesting? Over a century ago, our distant relatives probably worked together, and now today we're working together again. I'm just amazed."

Stephen could not ignore the eagerness in Reine's voice. Her enthusiasm sent a thrill through him that he could not deny.

"You'll have to let me know what you discover in your research. You should have more time now to investigate such historical events."

"Oh?"

"Despite all the complications in my schedule this past week, I am happy to announce that I was able to accomplish one important task. I have hired Lynn Patterson to take over full-time as nanny to the children starting next week."

"You have?"

"Yes. Now you'll finally be able to get back to a reasonable work schedule once again. Plus, you'll have the time and means to take a graduate class or two."

He tried to read the expression on her face but he could not. He only hoped that she was happy about his news. "Lynn has promised to take the position until she goes to college next fall. That should give me plenty of time to settle into our new schedule."

"New schedule?"

"Well, the boys will be starting school in a few weeks, and Sarah will be alone without her brothers for company. We all have new adjustments to make again."

He watched Reine chew her bottom lip. This was the permanent solution she had wanted, right? Why did he have the feeling that she was less than satisfied with the arrangements he had made?

She hugged Captain Morley's 1858 logbook and met his eyes. "I guess you won't need me anymore then?"

No, not need, but I want you more than ever, Reine. I want you in my life. This is not the end. It is the beginning for us.

He said the words to himself, but he was hesitant to say them aloud to Reine. He was not sure how she felt about him.

He inhaled a long breath. "Not as a nanny anymore, no. We are all very grateful for your help, Reine. I hope you will come by often to visit. The children will want to see you."

"Yes, of course. I'll want to see them too." She rose from her chair. "I'd better go."

"Wait, Reine." He reached out to grasp her hand. "I . . . may I call you sometime?"

"If Lynn can't watch the children? Yes, call me anytime."

"No, I mean, not that. May I call to see you?"

"To see me?"

"Perhaps we could go out to dinner or go to a movie?"

She smiled then, and he thought he saw a shadow leave her eyes. "Dinner or a movie would be nice. Yes."

Chapter Fourteen

He still hasn't called you?" Deborah slid onto a bench at the little beachside park and unzipped her insulated lunch bag. "I just can't figure it out."

Reine sighed as she took a seat across from her friend and gazed out at the powerful ocean surf. "There's nothing to figure out. He's not going to call me."

"Maybe he's gone away on a business trip." She shook her head. "No, I would have heard something. Jeremy hasn't mentioned a word about any trips Stephen has taken."

"He hasn't gone away, Deb. Just face it. He's not interested in me."

Deborah seemed to ignore her and bit into a roast beef sandwich. "I wonder what's going on."

"That's just the point. There is nothing going on." Reine sighed again. "I believe that men find me appealing only when they need something from me."

Deborah took a drink of water from her aluminum bottle. "Having such a pessimistic outlook is so unlike you and, anyway, you're wrong. Stephen cares about you, a lot. He's not like

Alan. Plus, he likes plain vanilla ice cream, just like you. I know my theory is correct. There's something else interfering with fate right now."

Reine gave her head a resolute shake. "No, it's been two weeks. We never had anything but a business agreement. That's all. It's over."

Deborah reached across the table and took a carrot stick from the dish Reine held out to her. "I haven't told you yet about there being another mystery to solve."

Reine rolled her eyes. "Please, Deb. Don't start."

"No, no. I'm serious. Mrs. Saunders has been buying unusual items at the market again. Things she's never gotten before. Artichokes. Unsalted butter. Some fancy special blend of European coffee."

Reine bit into her cheese sandwich, but it tasted like cardboard. She swallowed one bite and then wrapped the rest and put it back in her lunch bag. "Let's talk about something else. Is everything all ready for the garage sale on Saturday morning? Are we still meeting at the community hall at six o'clock to set up the tables?"

Deborah nodded. "You're not giving up, are you? You can't, Reine. Stephen Morley is your one true love. I just know it."

"No, he's not. I worked for him for a month taking care of his niece and nephews. He doesn't need me anymore. It's over."

"You're going to the softball competition and barbecue at his beach house on Saturday afternoon, aren't you?"

"I don't know anything about it, but I don't think so. I would feel really uncomfortable, I think."

Deborah reached across the table and squeezed Reine's hand. "I hate seeing you like this. Jeremy and I are going out for ice cream tomorrow evening. I'll ask him what's going on with Stephen. I promise to get to the bottom of this."

"Please, Deb. Just drop the whole thing. I want to move on with my life."

She could not understand why, on the night he told her he had hired Lynn Patterson as the children's nanny, Stephen had mentioned calling her for dinner or a movie. Why had he bothered to ask her when he had no intention of getting in touch with her? It had been two weeks since she had seen him.

The time seemed like a year. She missed Stephen so much that she could think of nothing else except him during most of every day, and she had not gotten a good night's sleep in that whole time. How was she going to forget about him?

Later that day, the telephone rang just as she was leaving her office. She jumped, and her heart fluttered as she anticipated Stephen on the line.

She forced the disappointment from her mind as she heard her grandmother greet her. With a deep breath, she made herself speak. "I'm just heading over to your house. Is everything okay?"

"Fine, dear. I hate to bother you, but I'm all out of butter. You know how your grandfather won't eat steamed broccoli without real butter. Would you mind stopping by the market to pick some up for us?"

"Not at all, Grandma. I'll see you in a little while."

In the nearly deserted Oceanside Market, Reine remembered the conversation she had had at lunch with Deborah earlier. Her friend had mentioned that Mrs. Saunders had bought unsalted butter when she purchased Stephen's groceries. *Who eats unsalted butter?*

She hurried from the store and did not see the man leaving the florist shop next door until he was less than a foot from her. Almost dropping the bag of butter, she sidestepped him just in time. "Oh, excuse me."

"Reine?"

When she looked up into Stephen Morley's dark eyes, she saw surprise and what appeared to be pleasure. She hoped it was not just wishful thinking. Swallowing, she chided herself for hoping for something more from their relationship. "Hello, Stephen."

"How are you, Reine?"

She could not ignore the huge bouquet of long-stemmed red roses in his arm. She tried not to speculate on the recipient of such beautiful flowers.

"I'm well. Thank you. How are the children?"

He nodded. "Fine. They're doing well." He looked down at the roses. "I'm sorry to have to rush, but I have dinner plans."

"Yes, I do too."

"I made reservations for six, so I really have to go."

"Of course."

"Tell your family I said hi."

"I will. It was nice to see you, Stephen."

"Yes, I'm glad I ran into you. Goodbye, Reine."

The whole conversation took less than a minute. As Reine stood on the street watching Stephen Morley hurry to his vehicle, her heart felt heavy. What had just happened? He had been in a rush and had little to say to her. She could not help wondering with whom he was going to dinner. Reservations? Roses? The person must be very special.

Reine stepped away from the row of glass display cases filled with turn-of-the-century photographs of life on the Outer Banks as visitors to the Nags Head Library and Community Center waited in line to view the new exhibit. Looking up from the crowded room, she saw Eleanor rushing toward her.

"A woman is waiting in your office. I asked if someone else would be able to help her, but she insisted on seeing you."

Reine handed her assistant a pile of brochures describing the new exhibit. "Just try to keep the lines moving."

"I will. I told the woman that we were very busy today, but she said it was important that she speak with you. I had to help her in through the side entrance."

Reine frowned. "She didn't use the front door?"

Eleanor moved closer to her and whispered, "The side door has a ramp."

Nodding, Reine smoothed her navy skirt and headed into her office. A woman with short, straight dark hair sat in a wheelchair and appeared to be gazing out the window at the smooth water of Roanoke Sound as Reine crossed the carpeted floor.

She held out her hand as the woman turned the wheelchair and looked at her. "I'm Reine Jonson. How may I help you, ma'am?"

Dressed in pale green slacks and a matching jacket over a white knit blouse, the slender woman smiled at Reine, and a faint scar across her left cheek crinkled. Her intense eyes under thick lashes studied her as she grasped Reine's hand and gave it a firm shake.

"Miss Jonson, it is a pleasure to meet you."

The woman's accent sounded elegant and cultured to Reine's ears. Although she tried not to stare at the visitor, there was a familiarity about the woman that she could not pinpoint. She wished the stranger would identify herself. Perhaps the name would jog Reine's memory.

"I'm sorry you had to wait. We opened a new exhibit today, and we have lines of visitors waiting to see it."

"I apologize for dropping by unannounced, but I wanted to come and meet the young woman about whom my grandson will not stop talking."

A warm smile broke across the woman's face. "I am Antoinette Madeleine Desmond Morley, Miss Jonson. I understand that you took very good care of my grandchildren after their nanny left."

Antoinette Morley. Stephen's mother?

Reine sat down on a nearby chair. "Mrs. Morley? It's very nice to meet you."

She noticed the scar across the woman's left cheek creasing as she smiled again. At least Stephen's mother had no trouble smiling. "Please call me Maddie."

Reine leaned forward in her seat. "Peter and Jonah and Sarah must be overjoyed to have you here. Are you staying at the house with them?"

"Yes, it is wonderful to be well enough again to enjoy my grandchildren. I was in a very serious accident just before Guy and Samantha were killed." A shadow crossed the woman's pale face. "I was unable to attend their funerals, as well as to help Stephen adjust to having three children in his home. I have been convalescing in a rehabilitation center near Paris until recently, and I finally received my physicians' permission to fly here to be with my family."

"I didn't know about your accident. I'm very sorry."

"I am much better." Antoinette touched the arms of the wheelchair. "My legs are still too weak to support me when I walk, but they are improving every day."

"Is there anything I may do to help, Mrs. Morley . . . I mean, Maddie?"

Her visitor nodded. "Actually, there is something, my dear. My reason for coming today is that Jonah requested I invite you personally to our house for dessert this evening. The children have a surprise for you."

"A surprise?"

The woman's intense eyes sparkled. "I am under strict orders not to reveal the secret, but Jonah did tell me to let you know that we will be serving vanilla ice cream. I hope that is a flavor you like."

Reine smiled in spite of her uneasiness that the invitation to the Morley house was coming from Jonah and his grandmother and not from Stephen himself. She knew she had to forget about him. Their working relationship had ended, and there was no hope for a future together.

Antoinette Morley reached out to clasp Reine's arm. "Stephen and the children have been rather preoccupied since my arrival almost two weeks ago. They have worked with diligence to see that I am comfortable and not left neglected, but I am afraid that they have stopped their customary routines to provide me with such wonderful hospitality."

The older woman's hand trembled, but her grip was firm and strong. "Now it is time for all of them to stop pampering me and to start living their lives again. Having you for dessert tonight will be the beginning. Please say you will come, Miss Jonson."

Reine forced a smile. "It's Reine. Please call me Reine, and yes, I will have ice cream at your house this evening." She could not help wondering if Stephen knew about his mother's invitation.

Reine noticed that Stephen's dark SUV was not parked in the driveway as she approached the beach house. When she turned off the ignition of her car, she sat for a moment and waited for the knot in her stomach to stop twisting. She did not understand why she was so nervous.

For a month, she had gone to the beach house on Morley Cove in Roanoke Sound almost every day. The place was familiar to her, but she was so ill at ease that she was nauseous. She was no longer certain what part she played in the lives of the Morley family. She was miserable that she wasn't a part of Stephen's life there anymore.

How could she have been so reckless as to fall in love with Stephen Morley? She had allowed herself to become attracted to a man who saw her only as an employee.

She remembered the bouquet of roses and the dinner reservation he had mentioned when she saw him on the street the previous evening. Her mood dipped to a new low. She tried to remember that she was there to see Jonah and the others.

With a heavy sigh, she walked up the steps of the beach house and knocked on the door. When Jonah answered, with Peter and Sarah right behind him, she forced a smile and convinced herself that she had to appear happy for the children.

"Come in, Reine. It is so good to see you." Antoinette smiled as she wheeled toward the little group hugging and greeting her all at once. "Mrs. Saunders set up the table in the breakfast nook in the kitchen before she left. Jonah insisted on having our dessert there."

The little boy's head bobbed up and down as he pulled Reine's arm and led her down the hall. "It's better than the dining room. That table's too big."

His grandmother nodded. "I agree. It is much easier to have a conversation when people are not sitting so far away from each other."

"Let's show Reine the surprise first."

"We have already discussed it, Jonah. First, we have our ice cream."

"I don't think I can wait that long."

"Yes, you can, *mon petit*. You are five now and old enough to be patient."

Jonah kicked the polished hardwood floor with the toe of his sneaker. "I don't like being patient. It's too hard."

Curiosity tempered Reine's profound disappointment that Stephen's place at the small table remained empty during the entire time they ate ice cream. The adults enjoyed fresh-brewed coffee as Reine wondered what sort of surprise caused both Jonah and Peter to bounce in and out of their chairs until everyone was finished eating.

"May I pour you another cup of coffee, my dear?"

"No, Grand-maman, please!"

Reine smiled at Jonah's pleading expression and shook her head. "I've had enough, thank you. I think I'm done."

"It's time, then?" Peter asked.

"You're ready to see our surprise?" Jonah asked.

"I'm ready."

Peter and Jonah slid down from their chairs in unison. As Reine rose from her seat, Jonah held up his hand.

"No, stay here. Wait for just two minutes while Pete and Sarah and I get ready. Then you and Grand-maman can come into the living room, okay?"

Astonished, Reine sat back down in her chair. She glanced at Antoinette, whose dark eyes sparkled with apparent knowledge of the secret the children were keeping.

While they waited, she helped Stephen's mother clear the table and load the dirty dishes in the dishwasher. Reine strained to hear any sound to indicate that Sarah and the boys were ready for her, but the house was quiet. Finally, she could wait no longer.

Antoinette met her gaze. "Shall we go in and check on them?"

Reine followed the older woman through the dining room and out into the hallway. Peals of laughter and children's voices filled her ears from the nearby living room, and her heart lost some of its heaviness.

The three Morley youngsters had lost and suffered so much in recent months. It was good to hear their childlike squeals of delight.

Stepping into the living room doorway, she felt her smile widen at the scene before her. In front of the fireplace on the area rug, all three of the children were tumbling and giggling and cheering as a small golden retriever scampered around them.

A puppy. Stephen had finally allowed the children to have the pet they had longed for.

Walking into the room behind Antoinette, she did not at first notice Stephen standing on the other side of the rug on which the children were playing. When she did, she felt her heartbeat quicken. He was leaning against the mantel, watching the antics of the group on the floor.

He straightened when he saw her. "Reine. I didn't know you were here."

Jonah's blond head snapped around to the doorway, and he grinned at her. "Look, Reine. Isn't this a great surprise? We have a puppy."

The little boy jumped to his feet and rushed across the room. "Come on. Come play with him. He loves to run and bounce and cuddle. He's just perfect, just what we wanted. Right, Pete?"

He pulled her toward the rug. "This is one of Teddy's puppies. Remember how I told you that Teddy was a dad now? This is one of his sons."

"Oh, he's adorable." Reine kneeled on the floor and tucked the edges of her tiered skirt around her legs. She reached out with her fingers to rub behind the little dog's ears, and he twisted his head to lick her hand.

Sarah squealed. "He likes Reine." She turned to her uncle as the puppy jumped into Reine's lap and wagged his tail. "Look, he likes her."

Stephen unbuttoned his jacket and leaned against the fireplace once again. "He is obviously a good judge of character."

Reine's heart gave a little leap at the sound of his quiet voice. She looked up at him, but the expression on his thin, handsome face was unreadable.

Jonah patted the golden retriever as the puppy bounced around on Reine's legs. "We have to choose a name for him."

Peter moved toward them. "We thought about calling him Teddy Too, you know, because he looks just like his dad except he's smaller."

"But I think we decided on something else." Jonah rubbed the puppy's ears with his fingers. "Doesn't he look like he's smiling? He's so happy."

Reine nodded. "He certainly seems as though he likes his new home."

"And we're so happy Uncle Stephen brought him here to live with us." Peter looked over at his uncle standing nearby, watching in silence.

Reine tried to meet Stephen's eyes. She wanted to tell him he was doing the right thing. The children needed a pet. It was obvious that they adored the little dog, but his gaze followed the puppy and his niece and nephews. Either he did not realize she was looking at him or he was avoiding her.

"We think we're going to name him Sunshine because he's so happy, and he has yellow fur." Jonah urged the little dog from Reine's arm back down to her lap. "We'll call him Sunny for short."

"That way we'll always have Sunshine and Reine, no matter what the weather is." Peter grinned. "That was Jonah's idea, Sunshine and Reine."

She smiled as Sarah climbed onto her lap and tried to catch the golden retriever, but the little puppy jumped out of her reach. With determined movements, he scrambled up Reine's right arm, across her shoulder, and onto the top of her head. With a paw on each of her temples, he sat there resting with his back legs braced on her shoulders.

The boys burst out laughing, and Sarah clapped her hands as the puppy seemed to enjoy the view from his new vantage point. Reine giggled along with them as she tried to hold still so the little dog would not slip and fall.

Jonah pointed toward her head. "Sunny must think he's a kitten climbing a tree, Reine. He's so silly!"

Keeping her head steady and balancing Sarah on her lap, Reine glanced up at Stephen, who had not moved from his position next to the unlit fireplace. What she saw at that moment astounded her.

Her breath stopped, and her heart leaped in utter amazement. Stephen Morley was smiling!

A thrill of delight rushed through her as she stared at him. His expression of amusement was broad and reached almost up to his sad, dark eyes. The tension on his face seemed to ease as he allowed himself to enjoy the simple pleasure of watching a puppy play with the children in his care. The deep lines etched in his forehead softened, and the dark circles under his eyes faded with the appearance of the genuine display of pleasure.

Reine wanted to laugh and cry all at the same time. Stephen was smiling. She had almost given up hope that she would ever see his face hold any expression that did not demonstrate seriousness, frustration, or pensiveness.

The joy she observed in him was pure and wonderful. She could only imagine what he saw and how he felt as he watched the puppy on its precarious perch, but watching Stephen smiling as he stood by the fireplace made her love him more than ever.

We must look ridiculous! She felt strands of hair, loosened from the elastic band at her nape, fall around her ears and cheeks as the little golden retriever readjusted his stance to keep his balance on her head and shoulders.

All too soon, Stephen stepped toward her and lifted the puppy from her head. As he squatted to set Sunny on the floor at his nephews' feet, his smile disappeared. In an instant, his face became somber once again.

Reine fought the overwhelming disappointment that washed over her. For a fleeting moment, she had witnessed a miracle, or something close to it; but then, just as quickly as it appeared, Stephen's brief expression of happiness vanished.

She set Sarah on the floor next to the two boys and rose on unsteady legs to a standing position. Life was so sad sometimes. She wanted to be happy about seeing Stephen smile. The love she had for him only increased at the thought that he was capable of expressing joy about frolicking puppies and laughing children, but that was the problem. She loved Stephen with all of her heart. She had known for a while, but seeing his smile had sealed that fact. She was in love with him, but he did not feel the same way about her.

Stephen was not in love with her. In fact, just the previous night, he had bought roses for and took someone else out to dinner. With a heavy heart, Reine got ready to leave.

Forcing a smile, she smoothed her skirt with the palms of her trembling hands and turned to Antoinette. "Thank you for inviting me for coffee and dessert. I have to go now." She looked back at the children on the floor. "I'm so glad you invited me to meet Sunny." She waved to the children as she started toward the door leading to the hall. "He's going to be a wonderful friend to all of you, I'm sure."

Antoinette smiled at her. "We would like you to join us here tomorrow after the Summer Fun activities in the village. The children would like you to come."

The children would but not your son. Reine forced a smile as she watched Stephen stride toward her.

"They're always talking about you." Stephen followed her through the doorway into the hall.

On unsteady legs, she looked back at him. "I miss the children too."

He walked with her to the front door. "Reine, I . . ."

"Yes?"

"Will you come tomorrow?"

"I don't know. The children have Lynn and your mother now."

He reached out and grasped her hand. "Please, Reine. I would like you to come."

You would? The sound of his quiet voice, the implication of his words, and the warmth of his touch mixed together to confuse her senses. All at once, her head began to spin, and her legs turned to rubber.

With reluctance, she lifted her gaze to meet Stephen's dark eyes. She saw no hint of the arrogance and self-assurance so typical in his demeanor. She saw only uncertainty mingled with expectation.

"Will you?"

As if she were moving in slow motion, she swallowed, nodded, and then pulled her hand away from his distracting touch. "I have to go now."

Stephen stood in the front doorway and watched Reine drive away from his house on Morley Cove. As he dragged a hand through his hair, disappointment washed over him and left him feeling empty and alone. Only the anticipation that he would see her on Saturday gave him hope that he had not lost Reine forever.

"She is a very special young woman."

He nodded as his mother wheeled toward him. "I know."

She lifted sculpted eyebrows above dark eyes. "Do you care about her?"

"I'm afraid I've fallen in love with her."

"That is wonderful, my dear."

He sighed. "She listens and understands me. She is intelligent and kind and patient. She's just perfect for me, but I don't think she feels the same way about me."

He recalled Reine's joyous laughter and the expression of approval on her pretty, slender face as she played on the floor with his nephews and niece and their new puppy. She had said very little, but he knew she supported his decision to give the children a pet. After all, the idea had been hers from the beginning.

His mother smiled and reached for his hand. "What makes you think she does not have the same feelings for you?"

He leaned against the doorway. "I don't know. Maybe she does, but I do know that she does not want to be tied down with a family right now."

"She told you that?"

"When I hired her temporarily, she made it clear that she did not want to take care of the children indefinitely."

"Being a nanny to someone else's children is a big responsibility. I think the two of you need to take some time to get to know each other."

He stared at his mother. "I want that more than anything, Mother."

She grasped his hand. "Reine is an intelligent, responsible young woman. Do not assume that you know what she wants. I am sure she is qualified to make up her own mind about such matters. Spend some time with her. Ask her out on a date, Stephen."

"I guess I'm afraid of the answer."

"You will never know unless you ask, my dear." Antoinette smiled. "As I said before, she is a very special person. You believed that by replacing her as the children's nanny, you would be able to forget about her. You thought that finding another childcare provider would solve your problems. But it didn't."

He shook his head. "It seems I have created more."

"That's because she is in love with you."

He looked at Antoinette as he considered her words. "How do you know?"

"I can see it in her eyes and in the way she looks at you."

"Do you think—"

"You have to talk with her." His mother smiled. "But do not wait too long, Stephen. You deserve to be happy."

Chapter Fifteen

Reine poked another pin through the decorative red ribbon and then through the blue cotton fabric of the cap in her hands. For a moment, her eyes drifted to the window of her grandparents' small living room, where she could see the glistening, smooth surface of Roanoke Sound in the bright, late afternoon sunlight.

"What's wrong, chickadee?" Her grandfather set his newspaper on his lap and gazed at her from his chair. "I don't think I've ever seen you look so glum."

She sighed and forced a smile. "Nothing's wrong, Grandpa. I'm just trying to get these sailor hats ready for the Morley children for tomorrow's ceremony."

Footsteps on the front porch interrupted her thoughts, and she looked up as Niles opened the screen door and strode into the living room. With one hand he lifted their grandfather's old canvas fishing hat from his head while holding a white plastic bag in the other.

"It's a beautiful day out there. Why is everybody sitting around in here?" He held up the plastic bag. "I hope Grandma hasn't planned dinner yet. I have a nice sea bass, all cleaned and ready to broil. The guest who reeled it in likes to fish but doesn't like to eat his catch."

Her grandfather leaned forward in his chair. "I haven't had sea bass all summer. You're finished awfully early today, aren't you, Niles?"

"I took a gentleman out on Oregon Inlet at dawn this morning as a favor to Stephen. He's a business acquaintance who had to go back to New York right after lunch. Hey, by the way, Stephen wanted me to remind you that you're all invited to the softball tournament and chicken barbecue at his place tomorrow after the Summer Fun activities in town."

Reine pinned the last of the ribbon to the nautical cap and picked up a spool of red thread. Her heart felt heavy as she worked. She would probably never attend any celebration at the Morley beach house again.

"It's a combination staff appreciation day and birthday party for Stephen's mother. Her actual birthday was earlier this week."

Reine snapped her head around to look at Niles. Her brother did not seem to notice her sudden interest.

"Do you remember Maddie, Grandpa? She mentioned just the other day when I saw her at the resort that she knows you from when she used to live here in Nags Head."

Her grandfather folded his newspaper. "Maddie Morley? Young Stephen's mother? Yes, of course. Has she moved back here to stay?"

"Apparently she was in a terrible accident and almost died a couple of months ago. When she pulled through, the doctors said she would need a lot of rehabilitation, but now she's better."

Niles grinned. "She's been helping out with the kids at the house and coming to the resort to look around and get to know the staff. She's really friendly." He turned to Reine. "By the way, next Saturday, Jonah and Pete want you to come fishing with us. Even Maddie's going. I'm sure that little chatterbox, Jonah, will tell you all about our plans for that day when you see him at the barbecue."

"I don't think I'll be going fishing."

"Oh, it'll be fun. Gwyneth and I are going, and Jeremy is taking Deborah."

Her grandfather lifted his eyebrows. "Gwyneth?"

Niles nodded. "Stephen's executive assistant. She's a little uptight and claims to hate fishing, but I plan to change all of that. In fact, I'm taking her for ice cream after dinner tonight. She likes butterscotch ripple, just like I do." A grin spread across his face. "I still can't believe that someone classy like Gwyneth is interested in a local like me, but we both enjoy butterscotch ripple, so we have that, at least, in common."

"I'm wearing my sailor hat to bed. I bet it'll make me dream about Captain Morley and his adventures." Jonah tugged on Reine's arm late Saturday evening on the porch outside the Morley beach house. "Will you tell me another story about him?"

"Come in and read the puppy book, Reine." Peter wound Sunny's leash around his hand. "Don't you want the puppy book, Jonah?"

"We don't have time for any book. You have fifteen minutes to scrub up before bedtime," Lynn Patterson said while she shifted Sarah, who was squirming and whining, from one arm to the other.

Reine watched as Peter struggled to keep control of the little golden retriever bouncing around at their feet. She held her breath when the nylon strap wrapped around Lynn's ankles.

Jonah pulled on Reine's arm. "I want a story, and I'm keeping my sailor cap on."

She smiled down at the little boy and patted his nautical hat. "I came to say good night, Jonah. It's late. You need to listen to Lynn."

Sarah wriggled in the young woman's arms. "Rock me, Reine."

Reine swallowed as Sunny made another turn, and Lynn stumbled against the puppy's leash. She reached out to help Peter untangle the length of blue nylon.

"I promised Mr. Morley that I'd help the boys bathe and get ready for bed before I left," Lynn said with a sigh. "I gave Sarah her bath before the party, but she's tired now and wants to go to sleep."

Reine nodded in understanding. "You can't do everything. Let me take Sarah."

"Then will you read to us, Reine?"

"I'll read the puppy story, Jonah, but you have to hurry." Lynn took the little boy's hand. "You're supposed to be in bed soon."

With a few verbal protests, the boys accompanied Lynn upstairs. Reine followed them as she held their little sister, who had settled against her shoulder.

She entered the nursery and sat down in the familiar and comfortable rocker she had used so many times in the past as she held Sarah while she slept. In the quiet room, Reine rocked the little girl and tried to ignore the emptiness in her heart.

The day had been wonderful. The weather was hot and clear. Crowds of residents and participants had attended the Summer Fun celebrations in the village. Afterward, enthusiastic staff members of Morley Cove Resort and friends of the Morley family had enjoyed a series of softball games down by the waterfront. Then everyone had sat down to a delicious dinner of barbecued chicken, cold salads, watermelon, cake, and ice cream under a large airy tent near the grove of weathered loblolly pine and oak trees on the edge of the Morley property.

She could not have asked for a better day. The Morley children had not hidden their excitement about seeing her, and Antoinette had gone out of her way to make Reine feel welcome, but still, she felt miserable. Stephen had not spoken with her for more than a few moments all day.

In his defense, he had treated his guests with superb hospitality. Without obvious effort on his part, he had welcomed them with engaging conversation, served cold drinks and tasty snacks, and paid courteous attention to everyone's needs.

Recalling Stephen's aptitude as a charming host brought Reine little comfort. Being at the beach house again reminded her of how unfulfilled her life seemed at the moment. Before she met the Morley children and fell in love with their aloof and handsome uncle, her main goal had been to begin her graduate studies and to advance in her career. She was not sure if that aspiration was important to her anymore.

If she had to choose between going back to school and starting a life with Stephen and his family, she was not sure which one she would pick. Tears filled her eyes as she looked down at Sarah asleep in her arms.

"I remember the first time you came to the house. When I watched you rock Sarah, you looked so serene and relaxed. I thought, by some miracle, you had been sent to help me with the daunting task of raising my brother's children."

At first she thought she'd imagined the sound of Stephen's deep, quiet voice. When she turned her head and saw him standing in the doorway of the nursery, her heart missed a beat.

"You're still working miracles with her."

Reine shook her head. "It's no miracle. Just a tired little girl and a wonderful old rocker."

"My mother used to rock my brother and me to sleep in that same chair."

"Maybe Sarah feels the connection, and it gives her comfort."

He strode across the room in his khaki shorts, running shoes, and dark green polo shirt embroidered with the Morley Cove Resort logo. "Is she asleep?"

Reine nodded and rose on unsteady legs from the rocker. "I was just going to put her in her crib."

"Let me." When he reached for his niece, his fingers brushed Reine's arm.

Despite the warmth his touch still made her feel, she shivered. Inhaling a long, deep breath, she watched him cover Sarah with a lightweight cotton blanket.

"She looked so cute in her little sailor hat today." He touched the sleeping child's cheek with the tip of his fingers before turning to Reine. "And the boys were handsome in theirs. Thank you."

"Jonah wanted to wear his captain's cap to bed."

"Don't tell me you let him."

"I didn't see the harm."

He lifted his brows in the dim light. "You never do. You spoil him. All of them."

"No, I don't."

"Yes, you do." The corners of his mouth turned up into a tentative smile. "But according to my mother, it's not spoiling. It's caring."

Reine smiled back at him. "It surprises you that your mother and I agree?"

"Oh, no." He followed her out of the nursery. "My father was the strict one. As I recall, Mother tended to give in to my many childish whims."

She laughed as he closed the door. "I can't imagine you with whims."

"I had some, and they annoyed my father." He walked next to her toward the stairs. "I've been trying to raise the children with the same strict rules that he used to discipline Guy and me. I'm afraid I may have been harsher at times than necessary."

"Don't be too judgmental, Stephen." She touched his arm as they reached the bottom of the wide staircase. "Toward yourself or your father. You both thought you were making the right decisions for your family."

"I'm trying every day to get this parenting thing right." He sighed. "Do you have a few minutes? There are some papers in the study I'd like you to see."

She wanted to leave. She wanted to head toward the front door and go home to her tiny, safe apartment. It was so hard to be near Stephen and not to be able to tell him how she really felt; but, instead, she walked toward the study and entered ahead of him.

He brushed past her as he approached the desk, and then touched her shoulder as he leaned to pick up a manila folder on one corner. "These are from my mother. Family statistics and historical background."

"Do you still want me to continue researching your family history?"

"Yes, unless you're too busy right now." His dark eyes met hers. "Before you start arguing, I plan to pay you for the time you work on it."

He continued to rest his hand on her shoulder. She swallowed as his nearness made her thoughts race. "Maybe you should ask someone else to complete the project."

"Why? You're the best in the area."

"It's just that, under the circumstances, you may prefer to work with another researcher."

She heard his sharp intake of breath. "What I would prefer is to work with *you*, Reine."

She raised her gaze to meet his intense dark eyes. "You said you'd call. You haven't, not once in more than two weeks. I thought you . . ." Her words trailed off into silence as tears blurred her vision.

She watched him set the folder back on the desk, and then he cupped her cheeks with his hands. "You're right. I'm sorry, Reine. I've been so busy with my mother arriving and trying to get the children settled with Lynn."

He leaned down and kissed her forehead. "I've thought about you constantly. I was late getting here last night because I tried to call your apartment to talk with you. I had no idea you were here having ice cream with my family."

"But what about the roses you were buying the other day and the dinner reservation you said you'd made? I thought you had a date." She blinked back tears. "I thought there was someone else."

He shook his head and brushed her cheeks with his thumbs. "I was in such a hurry that evening. I wanted to stay and talk with you, but the children were waiting. We were taking my mother out for dinner to celebrate her birthday. I had a date, yes. I was spending the evening with my family."

He smiled. "There is no one else, Reine."

Her skin tingled from his touch. She was not sure she understood what he was saying.

"I have something to tell you, something that is more difficult than anything I've ever done."

She swallowed. "What is it?"

He moved his hands to her shoulders. "I've wanted to call you every day, but I also wanted to be sure that what I was feeling was more than relief that I had someone competent and caring to help share the problems of raising three children."

Her voice was a whisper as his gentle caresses warmed her shoulders. "I was happy to do what I could for them."

He smiled. "Yes, I know you were, and I'll always be grateful for your generosity in making the children's transition here as easy as possible. As you and I began to spend more time together, and as our relationship grew into a wonderful friendship, I started to feel an attraction to you."

He slid one hand forward and used the pad of his thumb to trace her jawline. "I miss seeing your smile and hearing your laughter. I've come to realize that I do *need* you; but even more than that, I *want* you to be a part of my life, a permanent part."

She shivered at the touch of his thumb on her chin. "What are you saying?"

"I'm probably doing this all wrong." He cleared his throat. "You see, I've never been in love. I'm not sure what to say or how to act, but I know I would like more than anything to have your name next to mine someday on that Morley genealogy you're compiling."

She blinked. "My name?"

"Reine, darling, I love you. I don't know if you feel the same way about me or if you ever can, but I love you."

His words were hurried as he continued. "I know how important your work is at the library, and I never want you to give up your plans to go to graduate school. I want to help you follow your dreams."

"Oh, Stephen." She slid her arms around his neck. "I think I've loved you since the day I tried to convince you to donate your old furniture to the library fund-raiser, but I knew for certain when Sunny climbed on my head last night."

His dark eyes widened in question. "Sunny, the puppy?"

She nodded as her heart soared. "Yes, because that was the first time I saw you smile. It was the most wonderful sight I'd ever seen. I knew then that I loved you, Stephen."

His eyes darkened, and then he lowered his head until his lips touched hers. His kiss was light and tender and full of the love she had always hoped she would find. When he lifted his head and looked down at her, his eyes were sparkling.

"Really? It was the smile?"

She nodded. "At that moment I realized that my biggest

dream was to spend the rest of my life with you and to help you raise your three children."

"That would make me so happy, Reine." He wrapped his arms around her waist and urged her toward him as he brushed his lips across her cheek.

She sighed. "When we decide to plan our wedding, you know that Jonah is bound to have all sorts of ideas for it."

She heard Stephen's chuckle rumble from somewhere deep inside of him. In his strong arms, she felt comfortable and peaceful and full of hope.

"The child will most likely insist on your carrying wild-flowers in your bouquet and Sunny being in the wedding pictures."

"And he'll want us to have an ice cream sundae buffet at the reception with unlimited servings and all sorts of gooey toppings."

He kissed her again. "If we leave it up to Jonah, the guests will eat for hours and hours and still have room for the ice cream dessert with huge pieces of cake. Probably chocolate with orange frosting."

Reine laughed. "And we won't mind at all, as long as there's plenty of just plain vanilla for the bride and groom."

He wrapped his arms around her and smiled. "Yes, lots of it. We'll make sure there is always a big supply of just plain vanilla to celebrate every important event we have for the rest of our lives."